The Chosen

The Council of Shadows Series

The Chosen

William J. Simpson

Prominent Books

Editing & Layout: Writer Services, LLC (WriterServices.net)

ISBN 10: 1-942389-15-9
ISBN 13: 978-1-942389-15-6

Prominent Books and the Prominent Books logo are Trademarks of Prominent Books, LLC

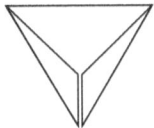

So many people helped me with this book! Too many to list individually, but you know who you are. Test readers, editors, artists and more! Everything you did has made this a reality. I am forever grateful!

Special Thanks to My Parents:
Bill & Karen Simpson

No matter the endeavor, they have supported me through and through.

Map Art: Diana Aitken—such an amazing and talented artist made my world a reality!
@dna.paint

And

Thanks to Writer Services. I wouldn't be here without the countless hours and time put in to get this book to where it is!

Table of Contents

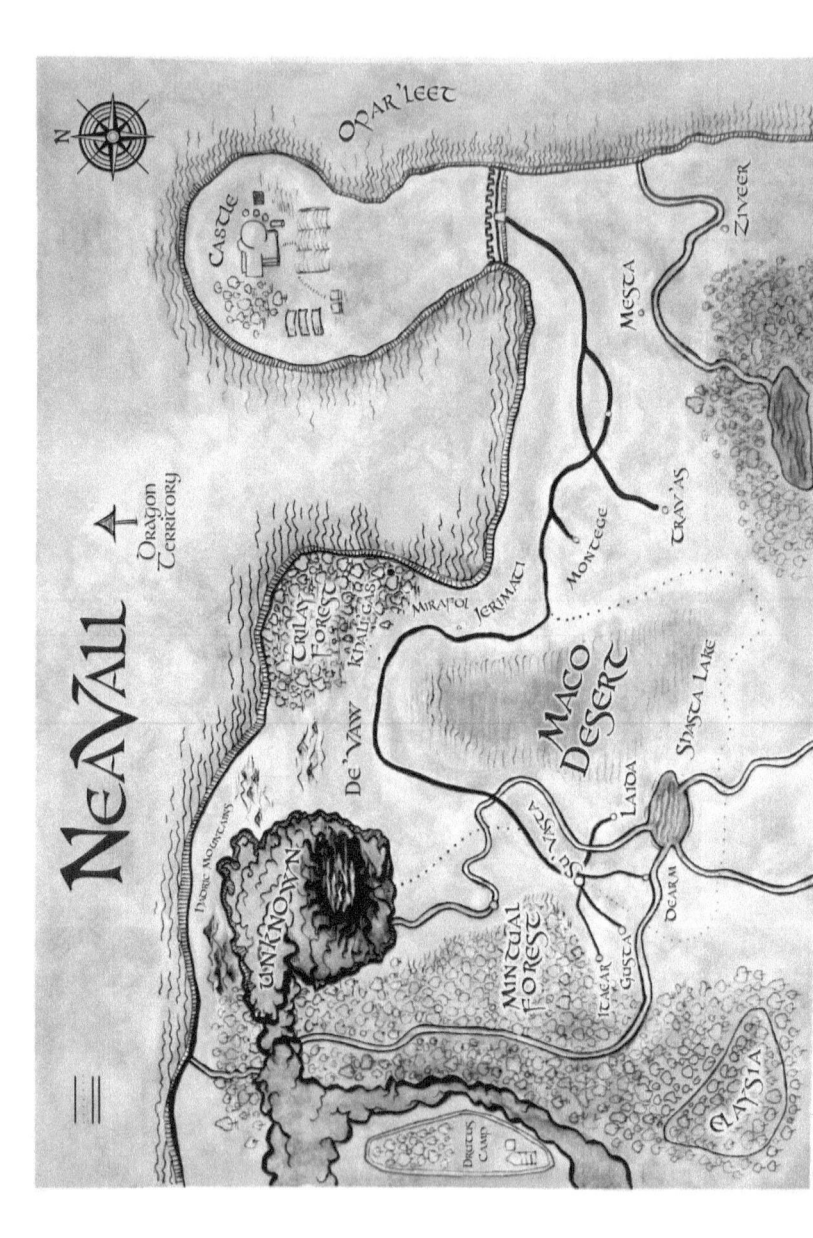

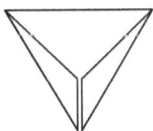

I'm not an artist. Give me a pencil and I'll draw you a stick figure, but give me a pen and I'll give you the world.

—WJS

Prologue

The air was crisp as the sun slowly settled behind the horizon. Its final goodbye recognized by the streaks of light cast across the ground. A lone dragon soared through the air at a lazy pace, the remaining sunlight reflecting millions of tiny colors off his scales. The wind was strong, causing ripples to permeate through his wings. His tail moved back and forth, keeping his body steady. Two horns shot out from the back of his head and curved towards his tail.

The dragon tilted his body downwards. As he came closer to the ground, he saw many black dots below him. He flew towards them, curious. A whistling noise pricked at his ears. The sound grew louder and louder.

The dragon released a stream of fire at the group of black dots as he noticed they had become arrows. They were flying directly at him. The fire incinerated many of them, but another volley was already coming at him. He beat his wings as hard as possible to try to dodge the second cluster.

It was too late; thousands of arrows made contact with his body. The dragon roared. His scales provided good armor, but there were too many. His wings were shredded as arrows sliced through them. Some of them managed to pierce the softer, vulnerable parts where his scales met. The pain ripped through his body as he began to go limp, his wings giving out. He fell.

The impact of this sizable creature was like an explosion, sending hundreds of pounds of dirt, brush and rocks some fifty feet in the air in all directions. The impact shook the ground. The trees trembled, sending a group of birds scattering skyward. Blood poured from his wounds.

A dark shadow slowly rose before him. The dragon blinked once, and death came over him as a blade slid straight into his head.

The Dark Ages had started in NeaVall. Dragons had been revered as the Supremes, until now. When the first dragon fell, the land erupted into chaos.

Over the next few years, dragons were continually hunted and killed. The responsible parties were never found. Finally, a decision was made. The thirteen rulers were called together to meet in Khali'Gas.

It was a dark night when they met. Thirteen robed men stood in the clearing in Trilay Forest. They all looked up as a thunderous noise erupted in the sky. A massive dragon landed in the clearing, causing the ground to shake. He was all black, but his scales reflected every little bit of light that hit them. He had a long tail and massive wings. His neck had spikes running up to the top of his head where huge horns curled back. His eyes blazed blue.

Each one of the thirteen bowed. "Karn," they all said with respect.

Karn lowered his head to acknowledge them. *What has been happening in the land has gone too far.* Karn's voice filled each one of their minds. His voice was deep with a hint of a growl. *I have summoned you all secretly. The dragons are leaving.*

An instant feeling of nervousness could be felt. The thirteen looked at one another, but they dared not speak.

We are leaving. However, we have decided to take thirteen people with us. We will teach these thirteen our knowledge. When they are ready, they will return to cleanse this land. They will help repair it, bringing it back to its former glory.

Once this is done, the dragons will return. Tonight, I am going to cast a spell. This spell will mark thirteen people at random—one from each of your towns.

They all bowed in agreement. Karn walked forward towards the center of the field. He lowered his head just above the ground, his scales shimmering as he blew an opaque mist from his mouth. The mist gathered into a sphere as he closed his mouth and backed away. The sphere began to shine brighter and brighter and then exploded upwards into the air. When it reached the sky, it shattered into thirteen smaller spheres of light and shot off in different directions.

In six months, those thirteen are to gather here. As a warning, if anyone arrives with a fake mark, they will perish. His eyes flared, and a feeling of importance fell over the others.

Throughout the next month, the Thirteen were marked and sent on their journey.

Six months had since passed, and thirteen smaller dragons sat in the clearing awaiting them.

A man walked into the center of the clearing, the dragons making a semi-circle in front of him. He bowed and removed his hood. The dragon on his far left moved up to him.

Show us your marking.

The man rolled up his sleeve. On the inside of his forearm was a mark. It was a triangle, the tip facing his hand. Inside, two lines came from the back corners to meet a third line, closest to the tip. On the backside was the Roman numeral for one.

The dragon bent down and touched the symbol with his nose. The symbol flared a bright white light. The dragon bowed to the man.

Thank you. Let us be off.

The man climbed on the dragon, and off they went. Over the next couple hours, eight more people arrived and went through the same ritual, but each of their markings had a different Roman numeral.

The tenth man arrived. He walked up to the center of the field. Four dragons remained—one directly in front of him, one on his left and two on his right. The dragon on the far right stepped forward.

Show us your marking.

The man revealed his arm, the symbol showing the Roman numeral for nine. The dragon stared down at the symbol.

That is your marking?

The man nodded, his body starting to shake. The dragon could sense his nervousness. He bent down and touched his nose to the symbol. This time the symbol flared red. A blinding light filled all of Khali'Gas. The man let out an ear-piercing scream. When the light faded, all that remained was a pile of clothes. Together, the dragons roared, fury exploding within them.

The remaining four arrived one by one shortly after. As they arrived, the dragon touched their marks. They flared white, and together they left. As the thirteenth flew away on a dragon, Khali'Gas went silent. There was no evidence of what had transpired.

The Thirteen were called the Chosen.

Ten years passed when they finally returned. The

land had worsened. They attempted to repair it to no avail. A plot was set in motion, and the Chosen disappeared, considered dead.

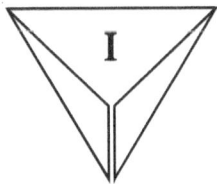

I

Llider sat crouched in the underbrush of the Trilay Forest. He was motionless, a wooden bow held in his hand. About thirty yards away stood a large deer grazing in the open. Llider slowly reached behind into his quiver, which rested on his back, and pulled an arrow from within. He notched the arrow and drew back the string, keeping his arm steady. He took aim, careful to aim for an instant kill. He slowly let out his breath, his arms steady, and released the arrow. It flew through the air with a soft hissing noise and not moments later lodged into the deer's neck.

Llider stood up and slipped his bow around his back. He walked into the clearing and stood over his prey. The deer was completely limp. He pulled the arrow out of the deer, causing blood to erupt from the wound. He knelt down and wiped the arrow in the grass, removing the blood, and replaced it back into his quiver.

The sun was fading fast, so he knew he needed to hurry. Being in the woods past dark was not wise. Plus, having a fresh kill, the smell was bound to attract bigger prey at night. He quickly field dressed the deer.

When he was done, he looked around the clearing and realized he was in Khali'Gas, the sacred land of the dragons. The area was flawless. Each tree had been burned in a perfect circle with no flaws. The grass remained one length—never too long or too short and never dried out or too moist. It was the perfect place for all wildlife to graze.

Khali'Gas always made him feel weird. A nervous energy always seemed to pulse through his body when he was there. His arm started to twitch as he looked around. He reached up to rub his arm, shaking his head as he tried to rid himself of the strange feeling. This revealed his birthmark.

It was very unique. It started on his shoulder creating a half spiral and wrapped around his arm once, ending right above the back of his elbow. It wasn't anything too peculiar except for the shape. In fact, it was almost impossible to see because it was only slightly darker than his skin color. Other than that, Llider was fairly normal. He stood about six feet tall and had dirty blonde hair that covered his shining green eyes. He was in great shape having grown up working on a farm.

Realizing the sun was falling faster and faster, he shook off the feeling and took the rope from his shoulder, unwinding it. He tied a knot in one end creating a loop. Then he took the other end and tied the deer's four legs together, tightening the rope so it was fairly short, just enough to drag the deer right behind him. He took one last look at Khali'Gas and made his way out of the clearing, back into the woods.

The deer, being bigger than he expected, made his return slower than he had hoped. He was only at the edge of the forest when the sun disappeared behind the horizon, causing rays of pink and orange to scatter throughout the sky. Llider decided that the best place to set up camp was right on the edge of the forest before the clearing. He unraveled the rope from his arm and threw it over a tree branch. He grabbed both ends and pulled down until he could comfortably hang freely without the branch breaking. Satisfied that the branch wouldn't break from the deer's weight, he let go of one end, tied it to the deer and hoisted the deer above the reach of other predators. The loose end was pulled and tied on a small root sticking out of the ground.

Once that was complete, he picked up some loose brush and placed it in a pile on the ground, surrounding it with rocks. He pulled out his knife and hit it against another rock, spraying sparks on the brush until a flame appeared. For the next few minutes, he nurtured the fire, blowing on it lightly and placing small sticks and pine needles in the small flame. When he got the fire up to a decent size, he kept it going by placing larger sticks on top.

He sat down beside the fire and, using his knife, shaved the end of a stick into a point. He then pulled out several pieces of raw meat from the pouch tied to his hip. He skewered them and placed the meat over the fire. He rotated the meat for several minutes, and when it was cooked to his liking, he pulled it off the fire and quickly devoured it so the smell would not attract animals.

After his meal, he gathered dirt and swept it on the fire, extinguishing it. Then he found the nearest climbable tree. Scaling it quickly, he found a spot where two branches connected, too high for curious animals. He positioned himself on the branches and then tied himself down. He lay down and closed his eyes, listening to the night's music as he drifted off.

The night seemed to last forever. He was awoken many times by passing animals and odd noises throughout the forest. Finally, he was able to fall into a deep sleep.

His dreams were very unusual. *First, he was the King of NeaVall. Then, instantly, he was roaming the desert in search of something, and a swirling red mist appeared in front of him. He laughed, unthreatened. As he moved closer, the mist solidified into the shape of a bear and lunged at him. Llider threw his hands over his face and screamed, falling backwards out of his dream.*

He instinctively tried to sit up but was restrained by his ties. Coming out of his dream, he blinked furiously and rubbed the sleep away. When he could see clearer and his focus came in, he laughed. "Just a dream." He untied his restraints and climbed down the tree.

The sun was just starting to rise, so he decided to pack his things. He made sure the embers from the fire were completely out and cleaned up anything that was left over. He threw his quiver and bow around his back and then went over to the deer still hanging safely in the tree. He untied the knot and lowered it to the ground. He then shortened the slack between himself and the deer and started his way home.

He made his way over the land separating Mirafol and the Trilay Forest fairly quickly. He traveled for the next two days out of the forest, and by early morning of the third day, he could see smoke rising in the distance from the town. He made his way towards his house, which was at the most southern part of town. He passed many places including the blacksmith, butcher, the tavern, some public lodging, and some few random traders. He nodded to many of the people he passed. He grew up in this town, so most people knew him as a mischievous little kid. He was much better now, but that label had stuck. Regardless of his label, everyone loved him. He was always helping nowadays and made everyone's life easier.

When he finally arrived at his house, his father, Tere, was outside chopping wood.

"Welcome back!" he said heartedly. "I see you were successful, which is excellent; we just finished the last of the other meat!"

Llider smiled as he replied, "Yeah, it took me a few days, but I finally got him. I found him in Khali'Gas. I seem to have good luck there all the time."

Tere frowned. He always hated when Llider went near that place, much less kill an animal in it. Although weird things were not proven to happen there, there were many stories, and these stories were believed as it was a sacred place. Tere left the matter alone, hid his anxiety and put on a smile as he walked over to Llider.

"Let me have that," he said as he took the deer from him. "I will handle it from here." He paused and looked the deer over. "Damn she's a beaut'. You did good this time; she's huge!" He smiled with approval and walked off, disappearing behind the house, dragging the deer.

Llider let a small laugh escape from his mouth as he looked at his house. It was very simple. It had a porch that went the length of the front, and there were two windows on either side of the front door. Inside were three rooms—a kitchen, bedroom and a little sitting area downstairs. A flight of stairs led up to Llider's room. It had a single bed and a few shelves, but what Llider liked about it was the window that surveyed the land behind the house. The land seemed to go on for miles until it disappeared into the horizon. It was home.

He made his way inside, leaving his boots, bow and quiver outside. The smell of meat and freshly baked bread greeted him at the door. He walked into the kitchen to find his mother, Celia, standing over the counter. She must have been working since early that morning; sweat was beading down her forehead. Fresh bread was cooling off on a table in the corner, and she was just putting the finishing touches on the meat. Her hands and arms were covered with flour. Despite this, she was still beautiful. She had a slim body and was good height for a woman. She had long blonde hair and soft blue eyes.

She turned around and jumped at the sight of Llider. She ran over and threw her arms around him, holding tightly. "I'm so happy you're back. You had me worried."

"I've been gone for less than a week, Mother," he replied, but she paid no attention as she continued hugging him. When she finally released him, he could only smile though he was now covered in flour. "Do you need any help?" he asked.

"No, I'm fine. Dinner is almost ready. I just have a few more things to do. Why don't you go get washed up and get your father?"

He agreed and turned to leave as she returned to her masterpiece. He went to his room where he grabbed a new set of clothes. He then made his way outside to the washroom located beside the house.

Inside was a basin with a pitcher of water next to it. In the corner was a tub filled with freshly warmed water. He smiled at the sight knowing his mom must have been expecting him, or just hoping. He didn't mind either way as long as it was there. He quickly stripped his clothing and sank into the water. He lathered a washcloth with soap and cleaned his entire body. When he was fully rinsed, he got out of the tub and dried off.

He threw on his fresh clothes and made his way to the back of the house to find the deer hanging by its hind legs. The head had been removed and the body skinned.

He found his father on the other side of the deer sharpening one of the knives he uses to cut the meat off the body.

"Dinner is ready," Llider said.

"Be right there," his father replied, putting the knife down and making his way to the washroom.

Inside, the table was set. The meat sliced into small strips and slices of bread with butter were placed on a plate. It was delicious. Llider and Tere tore into the meat and devoured slices of bread while Celia watched them, shaking her head disapprovingly. Once she thought it was safe to get some for herself without her hand being mistaken as food, she helped herself to her share. They ate in silence until each one had been more than satisfied.

Tere sat back with a huge sigh of relief. "You do know what tomorrow is, right?" he finally asked while Celia cleared the table. Llider frowned and nodded, knowing exactly what tomorrow was. Tomorrow, the recruiters from the king's army were coming to pick up the young men who had been drafted the previous year. There was Oli, twenty years of age, Heruki, sixteen years of age, and himself. Llider had been lucky enough to not be drafted for this long, but it was inevitable this time. "Are you all packed and ready to go?" Again, Llider just nodded, his expression showing his resentment.

The soldiers were supposed to come right before noon to the middle of town, and each boy was to have a horse and everything packed before their arrival. The trip was a long one. They were going to have to travel from Mirafol to the Kingdom of Opar'Leet. It was about a three-month trip on horseback. Llider was not looking forward to it, but it was either that or death. He chose the one that didn't involve the removal of his head.

When the conversation was obviously finished, Llider

left the table and made his way up to his room. His bag had been partially packed from before he left for hunting, but it seemed his mother had added a few things. She had added some meat that had been salted for preservation, a spare plate, fork, knife and a canteen for water. He set his hunting knife beside his bag and then rummaged through it. Satisfied with the two shirts and an extra pair of trousers, he tied it shut.

A few minutes later, he was out back where three horses were housed. He stopped in front of the first horse he came to. The horse's name was Sage, named by Llider when she was born. She was beautiful—white except for a black stripe that went down her nose. Her body was very muscular and fit for any work. Llider and Sage had a special bond since they had grown up together.

"Well, girl, tomorrow is the day we go on the long ride," he said, petting her nose. "Are you ready?" She whinnied in response and nudged Llider on the cheek. "Good! I'm going to need your strength!" He fed her some hay, ran his hand down her body and then left back to the house.

That night, Llider barely slept. His mind raced with the upcoming adventure on the horizon. Before he knew it, the sun was coming up, and it was time for him to rise.

The day went by fast. Llider did some chores around the house and helped with anything he could. He mainly just enjoyed his last day. When supper came, they all sat down to a hearty meal of steak and potatoes. Celia had gone down to the butcher to pick up some steaks for their last dinner together.

It was a very somber meal—Celia holding back tears between bites of food and Tere absorbed in his thoughts, or just not sure what to say. No one was in a joyous mood.

When there was no food left, Llider stood up, holding a dish to help clean up, and it was immediately ripped from his hands by Celia and set back on the table. Before he could respond, she drew him into the tightest hug, her tears finally breaking through and soaking his shirt. Saying nothing, he just hugged her back until she released him. "I'm gonna miss you so much," she choked out, her eyes swollen from crying.

"I'll miss you too, Mother. I'll come visit whenever I can."

She smiled. "You have a long day and need your rest. Off to bed with you." With that, she pushed him towards the stairs.

Once again, Llider dreamt. *He was riding his horse Sage down a dirt road when he saw a wagon being pulled by two horses coming his way. He could not see the people's faces but could tell that there was a man and a woman. He continued his pace, lazily admiring the rolling plains around him when a scream flooded his ears. His attention snapped back, and he could clearly tell the noise emanated from the woman on the wagon. He saw that a dark mist had appeared behind the couple, a sword sticking out of the man's body in front of a dark figure. A second figure started to materialize from the shadow of the wagon's cover. First an arm appeared, then a head, followed by the rest of the body.*

Llider drilled his heels into Sage's sides, urging her to gallop towards the wagon. When Sage didn't move, he cursed his horse, jumped off and sprinted as fast as he could towards the wagon. No matter how fast he ran or how hard he tried, he could not get closer.

He was suddenly forced backwards and onto the ground as a flash of light appeared from the woman's hand.

A hauntingly high-pitched shrill filled the air, created by the two robed men. The light disappeared, and the two men were gone. There was silence.

Llider stood up and could only watch as the woman fell out of the wagon, blood soaking her blouse. As she fell, her eyes connected with his. Llider stood transfixed; he felt as if he knew this woman. The connection was broken as her eyes closed and the last of her life evaporated.

He woke up, sweat running down his forehead. His left arm spasmed, and he gently massaged it until the muscle relaxed. It was very early, and the sun was just peaking over the horizon, casting lines of light across the ceiling. There he lay in bed, unable to fall back asleep. He thought over his dream for a little while, unable to shake the connection he felt. The woman, he knew her, didn't he? It felt so real.

The smell of bacon flooded his room, making him leave the dream behind. He threw his legs off his bed and sat up, the weight of the day hitting him like a ton of bricks. He pulled on his leather trousers, tucked his knife into his belt and then grabbed his white sleeveless shirt and pulled it over his head. Over that went his leather vest, which had been designed specifically with crossing metal loops on the back. Once satisfied, he grabbed his bag and made his way downstairs and out the front doors. He then slid on his boots and walked towards the horses.

There he saddled Sage and latched his bag to her side, making sure the weight was distributed evenly. Using her reins, he led her to a field so she could graze. He looped her reins around a post and walked back inside towards the kitchen.

Tere had already eaten, evidenced by a dirty plate on the table. Another plate, filled with eggs, bacon and a slice of buttered bread, sat on the table. Llider sat and scarfed down the food. His mother didn't eat a thing, just sat until he was done, picked up his plate and cleaned it. She could barely look at him, and when she did, tears built up in her eyes, but she would quickly look away and wipe them.

Knowing his time was short, he left the kitchen. Just before leaving the house, he turned to a large cabinet to the left of the door. Inside were many weapons. The first two were identical swords hanging side by side, an emerald in each hilt. They were family heirlooms that had been passed down for many generations. His father had given them to him on his sixteenth birthday, as his father before him had.

He grabbed one in each hand, twirled them both once and placed them through the metal loops on his back. The two swords crossed so each handle was sticking out above his shoulders. His bow and quiver were there, moved inside by his father he thought. He looped the quiver over his shoulder, holding the bow in his hand, and closed the cabinet doors.

Llider opened the front door, where his father had brought Sage and two other horses. Llider walked over to Sage and took the reins. "Good girl," he said as he patted her nose. She nudged him in response when the door opened again. Celia, looking like she had just finished crying, walked slowly out to the last horse. Tere held the reins steady as Celia mounted her horse. Once she was set, the other two did the same and headed off toward town.

They traveled in silence, an occasional sniff heard from Celia. The ride was brief, and before they knew it, they were entering the center of the town. Oli and Heruki were already there standing with their parents—Oli, with his mother and father, and Heruki with his father; his mother had died giving birth to him. Llider nodded to them both, and they returned the gesture. Llider and his parents dismounted their horses and just stood looking at each other for a moment.

Celia's eyes seemed to give up as tears flooded from them uncontrollably. She started to speak, her words interrupted slightly by her crying, "I can't believe you're going ... it's ... too soon." She pulled Llider into an embrace. It was a hug that he never thought he would be freed from.

"Don't worry, Mother, I'll be fine," he was finally able to say when she released him. "As soon as I can, I'll return to visit. I love you!"

"I...," she choked back tears, "love you too."

Minutes later, the thunder of horses could be heard coming towards the center. The group turned to look as twenty soldiers rode into the town's center in perfect formation and stopped. It struck Llider a little odd that so many soldiers came as escort, but dismissed it as the captain moved forward.

"We must leave immediately, so let's make this quick," the captain boomed, expressing no emotion in his voice. "When I call your name, move forward. Heruki, son of Tar." Heruki stepped forward. "Oli, son of Brin." Oli stepped forward. "Llider, son of Tere." Llider stepped forward.

One thing Llider noticed as the captain spoke was he barely glanced when each stepped up—never gestured towards them or made any indication that they existed. Llider looked at the other soldiers, and they looked as if they had no life in them either. Each soldier had a hollow stare, no personality, no emotion, nothing. They acted like statues.

"Let's move," the captain commanded, pulling Llider's attention back.

He turned to his parents. "Goodbye Mother." Then looked and nodded to his father, tears streaming from Celia's eyes.

"I am proud of you," Tere said, smiling as he clapped a hand on Llider's shoulder.

Llider smiled. "Thanks." He then mounted his horse and watched as Heruki and Oli did the same. Celia collapsed into Tere's arms but still looked at Llider. The soldiers turned their horses and started out of town. The three boys followed suit. At the edge of town, Llider turned and gestured a final wave goodbye and then continued to follow. As they rode, Llider kept glancing back at the town, hoping to get one final glimpse of his parents, until it finally disappeared into the horizon.

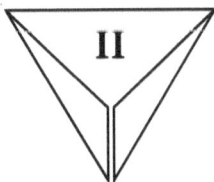

II

It was just after noon when they finally made it to the main road, traveling south at a decent pace. They were headed towards Dagmar but had to pass through Jerimati and Montege first.

Jerimati was a medium-sized town and was known for its uniquely crafted weapons. Although they were expensive, people everywhere traveled here to purchase them if they could be afforded.

Montege was an old Elven city. When the Elves disappeared, humans took it over. It was still a strange place though; the Elves had built odd buildings in the town. They were slanted in odd places, and the colors were very earthy tones. Some of the buildings had even been built into the trees. They had been changed through time since man had altered many of the buildings to look more normal, but it still held a sense of magic left over by the Elves.

The soldiers traveled in a very unique pattern—seven in front, seven behind and three on each side, the boys in the middle. It seemed to Llider that they were more prisoners than recruits. Soldiers these days had been doing odd things though, so Llider didn't consider it too much.

The two guys that Llider rode with were very different.

Heruki, the young red-haired boy, was very quiet and kept to himself. He was very good with daggers. He wore a plain white shirt along with black pants and boots, no armor though. Two daggers hung on each side of his belt. He rode a smaller black horse compared to Llider's.

Oli, on the other hand, was larger than Llider. He had long dark hair and a more muscular frame. He wore very decorated pants that were armored on the front of his thighs. His shirt was just a cover for the chain mail he wore underneath. On his side, hanging by a strap, was his axe. It was the weapon he loved. His father had made it for him when he was a little boy and had Oli's initials etched on the blade just above the hilt.

They traveled the majority of the day until the sun started to set. The captain stopped. "We will camp over there for the night," he said in his gruff, monotone voice, then led the group to a small area.

"You three," he said, flicking his wrist at the three boys, "gather wood and start a fire. You two," he pointed at two guards, "scout the area."

"Sir," They acknowledged and turned to comply.

The captain looked back at the boys. "Did I stutter?" he said, his voice filled with hatred. Having been distracted by his abruptness, Llider realized the captain wasn't used to saying things twice. They were in the army now. This was what was expected of him, regardless of the fact that they were still new recruits. This was their commander, and they needed to listen to him.

"No sir!" Llider quickly responded, dismounting his horse and going to look for wood. He motioned to the other two to do the same.

"Sir," he heard both Oli and Heruki say in unison as their feet hit the ground.

"Man, he's a hard-ass," Heruki said quietly as he and Oli caught up to Llider. Llider just nodded. They returned to the camp about twenty minutes later carrying quite a bit of wood and set it down in what seemed like the center of the camp. They gathered some brush and, using Llider's knife, sparked a flame. Oli nurtured the fire, and within a few minutes, they had a steady fire going.

Llider pulled out some of the meat his mother had packed. "Want some?" he offered to the other two. Oli grabbed a piece, but Heruki denied. Before he had even taken a bite, someone behind them cleared his throat, clearly attempting to get their attention. They all turned.

"When did I say you could eat?" the captain shot. "While you're with me, you'll eat when I say, piss when I say and sleep when I say. Otherwise, don't do a thing. Got it!" It wasn't a question. The three just gaped.

"My name is Gero. I am the captain of these men and now you sorry three until we arrive in Opar'Leet. I don't want to know or care what your story is, just do what I say, and we won't have a problem." There was a short pause while he let that sink in. The three nodded slowly. "I am going to test your skills and, when we arrive, recommend where you should be placed. We will start with you." He drew his sword and pointed to Heruki. Gero turned and walked into an opening where they had plenty of room to spar. Heruki, Oli and Llider stood and followed.

Gero stopped a few feet away, holding his sword steady. Heruki nervously made his way in front of Gero. He drew his two daggers, one in each hand, and stood in position. This seemed to amuse Gero as a sarcastic smile appeared, the first evidence of some emotion.

"We'll start slow then speed up." Gero lunged forward,

not starting slow as he had said. Heruki barely deflected it but recovered quickly and struck back at Gero's stomach. Gero blocked it with ease. Then with a much faster speed, he attacked Heruki once more. Again, it was barely deflected. For the next few minutes, they went back and forth until Heruki was bested and ended up with a cut on his arm, his dagger falling to the ground.

"That wasn't slow," Heruki pained as he pressed his hand into the cut.

"Could use some work," Gero responded, not paying attention to what Heruki had just said. "Your turn." He pointed at Oli. Oli stood up and walked to where Heruki was picking up his dagger. He placed it back in his belt, returning to stand next to Llider.

"Same thing," Gero commanded. Oli took his axe from his side and stood ready, knowing what was coming. Gero lunged forward once again with speed. Oli, prepared, deflected it easily and sent a counter-attack at Gero's arm. Gero sidestepped, parried the axe away and swung at Oli's other arm. Oli, recovering quickly, deflected him with ease and threw his other arm into Gero's body, pushing him back. He swung his axe at Gero's head but was blocked with surprising speed, and before Oli could react, he felt a searing pain across his arm.

"Could use some work," Gero repeated, a stunned look on Oli's face. "Next."

Llider stood up and switched places with Oli, giving him a passing glance. Gero gave the same instruction to Llider and lunged forward before Llider had drawn his swords. He dodged left and in the same motion drew his two swords from his back. Gero was already attacking again. Llider used both swords to block the sweeping attack, vibrations moving throughout his body. Gero bounced back and lunged again. Llider, more prepared this time, blocked with one sword, striking with the other. He almost struck Gero, but a knife appeared in Gero's other hand and blocked Llider's attack at the last second. Shock shot through Llider's body as the knife had appeared out of thin air.

Before he could think twice, the knife was flying at Llider's neck. He back-stepped just in time and raised his swords again to block Gero's slash. He realized that Gero was moving at a pace no human should be able to. Back and forth they went, Llider barely keeping up until Gero finally got him across the stomach.

"Could use some work," was all Gero said and walked away. Llider stood in silence as he watched Gero retreat back to the camp. Llider returned to where Heruki and Oli were standing, both with slightly stunned expressions on their faces.

"What the hell was that?" Oli's anger was breaking through as he covered his arm. "There was no gradient. He could've killed us. What if we weren't trained at all?"

"I don't know," Llider responded, a little breathless, "but did you see how fast he was? That wasn't human, and where'd that knife come from ... magic?"

"I don't know. I thought I was keeping track, but the knife appeared out of thin air. I'm not sure how I missed it."

"One thing I noticed," Heruki hesitantly started to say, "he showed no emotion, no effort, nothing. He gives nothing away. His eyes stay steady. I've never heard of someone being able to fight like that."

It was true. Llider thought that was a near impossible skill. He thought back on his fight with Gero and, sure enough, no emotion or facial movements. He usually used that to predict his attacker's next movements. That explains why he had so much trouble. But how? Llider looked around as they made their way back to camp and noticed none of the soldiers showed any facial emotion. They just did what they were commanded.

Exhaustion was settling in as the three found themselves a soft spot to lie down for the night. Before they pulled out their food, Llider glanced around and didn't see Gero in sight, so he scarfed down his food, Heruki and Oli following suit.

The sun was almost below the horizon; the only evidence being the few streaks of pink littering the sky. The main light now was the fire glowing behind them. Gero hadn't come back, so they assumed they were safe to rest. All three of them lay down, their weapons within arms reach, and drifted off.

A sharp pain erupted in Llider's ribs, forcing him awake. "GET UP!" Gero shouted. Llider heard muffled screams from Oli and Heruki as they too had been kicked. Llider sat up slowly, the pain in his ribs already aching. He rubbed his eyes and saw three dark shadows looming above, one directly over him and two beside the other boys.

"We have a lot of ground to cover, and you three are sleeping away. Get your lazy asses up, or we'll leave you behind." This was meant as a threat. With that, Gero walked away and mounted his horse, followed by the other two soldiers.

Pushing the pain aside, Llider eased up, the other two closely behind. They secured their weapons properly and jumped on their horses. Gero motioned for everyone to move out. Llider finally started to wake up and realized the sun hadn't even risen fully. It was just peaking over the eastern sky.

"Sleeping away, my ass," Llider grumbled to himself angrily, glaring at the back of Gero's head.

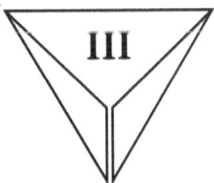

III

They traveled for the next twenty days, mainly on horseback, occasionally walking in front of the horses to give them rest. They camped at nightfall and then resumed at dawn. Some nights, Gero would spar with them. Other nights, the boys would spar by themselves. Mostly, they would teach each other how to use their personal weapons.

Llider and Oli started to teach Heruki how to use a sword. This went slow because it was longer and heavier than a dagger. Over time, he got better but still needed more work. They decided not to teach him how to use an axe yet. Llider was skilled in swords and bows, but he didn't know the correct technique on axe fighting, so Oli would spend time with that. Oli was fairly good with a sword but needed training with a bow. So while Heruki practiced with a sword, Oli practiced with the bow, and Llider would practice with the axe.

When the food ran low, Gero would send the three hunting. Llider would let Oli or Heruki shoot the deer to get practice with the bow. Occasionally, they had to hunt rabbit or another animal when they couldn't find any deer. Each of them were fairly good hunters, so they never came back empty-handed. However, since Gero had charged them with supplying food for the entire unit, it took a while.

When Gero sparred with them, he always said the same thing: "Could use some work." He never complimented them, never gave advice, and still no emotion. At the end of the first week, he tested the boys on the bow.

"Could use some work," was once again said when they finished the tasks given to them by Gero, even though they had all done extremely well.

When Llider could, he would watch the soldiers to try to figure out what was off, but when they noticed him, they would say something like, "What are you looking at?" and he would quickly look away. But other than that, the soldiers, except for Gero, rarely spoke. Llider didn't even think they really noticed him.

On the twenty-first day, they rode into Dagmar in the late afternoon. It was a very small town—smaller than Mirafol—but it was the last town before the castle walls, about six days away. Around the perimeter of Dagmar was a stone wall, with a single portcullis on each side of the town. As they rode up to the front gate, they passed by two soldiers, one on each side of the gate, who did nothing but nod to Gero. The town was very simple; it had one main street that went from one portcullis to the other with smaller roads branching off. Off the main road were shops, and these were surrounded by what looked like the housing.

They headed straight down the main road, stopping at a larger building, a sign hanging out front—The Rested Horse—burned into the wood. Gero raised his arm, signaling everyone to stop, and dismounted his horse. The soldiers and boys did the same. They left their horses outside and walked in. There was a single man standing behind the counter, reading. He was a portly guy in need of a good shave and some clean clothes. The inside was very basic. There were a couple of tables surrounded by chairs, and a staircase leading to the second level.

When he saw the soldiers, he quickly, almost sloppily, put the book down and asked in a choppy voice, "What can I get ya?"

"Eleven rooms," replied Gero bluntly.

"Eleven—" he coughed, regained his composure, then continued, "I don't have that many available, and how will you pay for these rooms?"

"How?" Gero responded, a menacing look flashing in his eyes. "I believe you will allow us to stay for free as we are a part of the king's army. And I really don't care if you don't have the rooms available. Make them available."

"Oh … yes, of course, sir. Sorry for the misunderstanding," the man said, clearly intimidated. "Right away. Please wait here for a second while I get them ready." The man left up the stairs, towards the rooms. A few minutes later, he walked back followed by a few families—three men and a couple women, all holding their bags. Not a single one of them looked at the soldiers but intentionally kept their eyes averted. The man returned behind his counter and said, "Right this way. I'll take care of your horses after I show you to your rooms." He led the soldiers upstairs. The soldiers entered their rooms; most were two to a room. Gero got his own room, and the boys had to share one.

"Two beds?" Llider observed as they entered.

"Well, the oldest should get the beds." Oli smirked at Heruki as he jumped on one of the beds, Llider quickly doing the same.

"Ugh...," Heruki groaned, expressing his annoyance.

"So what now?" Oli said as they put their stuff down.

"Well—" Llider started as the door was thrown open. Gero stood there.

"We continue our trip to the castle tomorrow. You may explore the town, but do not leave it. Got it?" Gero said sternly.

"Yes sir," they all answered in unison. Gero had already turned to leave.

"See, the man does have some humanity left," Llider joked. "Let's go find a place to get some food. I'd love a full meal." The other two nodded eagerly. They left the room and made their way down the stairs out.

"Which way to the tavern?" Oli asked the innkeeper.

"Take a left outside. You can't miss it," he responded nervously, obviously still shaken up by the encounter with Gero.

Outside, they turned left and made their way down the road, passing many shops. All the buildings were far more advanced than he was used to. They were made of stone and many had windows with flowerpots hanging in front. They were directly connected to each other, so there was no room to walk between them. Most were very dark, or closed; Llider couldn't tell. They passed a shop with smoke billowing out of the chimney. The sign out front said, "The Sturdy Hammer."

"Must be the blacksmith," Llider stated to the other two. It looked closed regardless of the smoke.

As they continued, they passed another building that had a weird smell emanating from it. In the window were four different skulls. It was very eerie. After a couple more minutes, they finally came to the tavern, a sign reading, "The Wily Gnome Tavern," giving it away.

The tavern was very plain. It had a long bar on the left side with stools for people to sit. There were many tables all around the floor, each with four chairs. A stage in the back corner for people to play instruments on was vacant at this time. In the back, near the middle, it had a staircase going to the second floor. Llider figured that was where the tavern keeper slept.

There were many people in the tavern, most drinking, some eating. Of all the people in the tavern, a small group caught Llider's eye. There were four of them. They were all sitting close together, talking. All of them wearing green robes, their faces were concealed by hoods. It was odd to be wearing that sort of thing. It definitely caught people's attention. Not many were sitting around them.

A girl holding a tray of drinks zipped by them. "Sit anywhere you like," she said as she went by. This pulled Llider's attention off of the strange folk momentarily. Llider noticed an empty table near the hooded figures and quickly led the other two towards it; something was drawing him towards them.

A few minutes later, after they had sat down, the girl returned, "What ya havin?"

"I'll have mead, your meat plate with corn," Llider ordered.

"Deer meat and potatoes for me, mead sounds good," Heruki said.

"Ditto on the drink, and I'll have pork and beans," Oli said last.

The girl nodded and turned to leave. "You three have coin?" she asked before leaving. Llider nodded again. "Good, because I don't want no funny business." And she left.

"This is an interesting town!" Heruki stated. "Nothing like Mirafol. Think it's because it's near the castle? Also, did you see that weird store with the skulls in it? What do you think that could be?"

"Hmm...," Oli thought, "a witch could work there, a

healer's supply, stuff for potions. Could be many things. It doesn't really matter because we won't have time to check it out. Llider?" Oli looked at Llider, noticing he wasn't even paying attention. "Llider?" Oli poked him.

"Huh ... what?" he said, coming out of his trance. "Oh, I don't know. What were you talking about?" Then, before Oli could reply, he said quietly, "What do you think of the four guys over there?" he motioned to the four men in hoods.

"Who cares?" Heruki replied excitedly, "Food's here!" The waitress had returned with hot plates of steaming food, placing them in front of each of the boys. They started eating almost before the girl had put the plates down. Llider didn't realize how hungry he was as he scooped bite after bite into his mouth. The girl left with a look of disgust as they all gobbled the food up.

"I'z too true!" a drunken guy yelled from a table near them when they were just about finished with their meals.

"What are you talking about?" said the guy sitting with him.

Clearly wanting people to listen, he raised his voice and started off on his story. "Well, a long time ago, NeaVall was a peaceful place to live. Errvery one lived and worked together. Dragons were even common. It wasn't uncommon for a dragon to be seen at least once a day, and sometimes people would even speak to the dragons." There was laughter from a few people in the tavern when they heard this. "I'ma not lying," he responded to the laughter as his elbow slipped off the table, barely catching himself. "It was when that damned thirteenth chosen disappeared from his position. And when those Drutas came into our world. Who knows what or who they are. All I know is they no good. Ever since they appeared, life has become a hell. And so I hear Phantoms are known to be roaming the land. I heard they are working with the Drutas as assassins...."

A guy stood up next to the drunk and said, "You stupid drunk. Stop telling this nonsense."

The drunk stood up straighter, swaying slightly and angrily replied, "I am not!" The guy pushed the drunk, causing him to fall back towards one of the strange robed men. Before the drunk could hit the robed man, he had moved so fast, the drunk missed him and fell, crashing to the floor. However, the man's hood had fallen, revealing his face. Llider quickly focused on the guy. His features were definitely odd. His face was very sharp. His cheekbones were prominent, and his eyes were alert. He had long blonde hair and, Llider noticed, pointed ears.

"An elf!" Llider said under his breath. Both Heruki and Oli looked at Llider confused. He nodded his head in the direction of the elf. Heruki and Oli both gasped as they noticed just before the elf had turned his head and re-covered his face.

The bar had gone quiet, the groans of the drunken man rolling around the floor was the only noise. Llider looked around. It seemed most people were focused on the drunk and hadn't noticed the elf. The elf nodded his head towards the door. The other three hoods stood up together and exited the tavern.

Without thinking, Llider shot out of the tavern after them, the hurried footsteps of Heruki and Oli behind him. When they got outside, the elf and his group were nowhere to be found.

"Damn!" Llider cursed, frantically looking around.

"Are you sure that was an elf?" Oli said, also glancing about.

"Positive. Humans don't look like that at all. Besides, he had pointed ears. I can't believe no one else saw him. Let's get back to the room. Too dangerous to talk about them here," Llider replied.

Right when they entered the room, Heruki burst out, "AN ELF! IN DAGMAR!"

"Ssssh! Don't say that so loud." Llider quickly put his hand over Heruki's mouth. "We don't want the soldiers to hear. Elves haven't been seen for a very long time. They disappeared about the time when the Thirteen Chosen returned. No one has seen one since. I should have known that's what those guys were. I mean did you see the way they were dressed? What could this mean? If they're reappearing, it must mean that something's happening." Llider went quiet, his mind racing. There was a silence between the three, all of them caught up in their own imagination. The silence was broken by a knock at the door, followed by it swinging open.

Gero stood in the doorway. "Go to sleep. We have a long ride ahead of us," and he shut the door.

Obeying what Gero said, they all got into their beds, Heruki wrapping himself up in blankets on the floor. The room went silent, but it was obvious that nobody was sleeping. Llider lay staring at the ceiling trying to make sense of what had happened earlier that night. The story the drunken man had told and the sudden appearance of Elves after all this time. Llider wondered who the Drutas were. He had never heard of them. He knew that the Thirteenth Chosen had left, but he couldn't figure out the connection between it all.

Before he knew it, he had dozed off and was dreaming again. *This time, he dreamt that he was riding through the forest with Sage. She seemed to know where she was going.*

Far off in the distance, Llider could see a bright light. He kept getting closer and closer to the light until he came to an area where the forest was thinner. Sunlight poured from the sky, illuminating everything around him. There were strange-looking trees all around. Groups of people were walking around. One guy was walking straight towards a tree. He stopped, reached out and pulled a part of the tree open and walked in. Stunned, Llider blinked his eyes until they focused. He was in a town, which was camouflaged into the trees and brush, almost impossible to see with a glance. The town had been built so well that you couldn't tell the difference without looking closely. He dismounted Sage and led her through the town. People were all around him, but he could not see their faces. He noticed one man running straight towards him. The man kept coming until he stopped directly in front of Llider, grabbed him on the arm and shook him. Llider tried to get away but could not break free. The guy just kept shaking him.

"Llider!" the guy said. "LLIDER!" he repeated with a more forceful voice. Llider opened his eyes to find Oli shaking him awake.

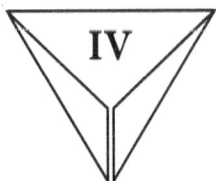

IV

It was early morning, and the sun had not yet risen when he was awoken by Oli. "You have to get up. Gero wants us ready to go immediately." The concern in his voice was almost tangible.

This annoyed Llider as nothing Gero did really made sense. But he got up and dressed. As he put his shirt on, he realized something. "Think this has anything to do with the elf last night?" Llider looked at the other two.

"Possibly," Heruki gave it some thought, "but I don't think anyone else noticed him. Or at least made him as an elf."

"I don't know. There were a lot of people there. I don't think everyone could have missed him," Oli said.

They left the room with their bags and made their way downstairs. All the soldiers were downstairs standing like statues, except this time there was an odd tension that filled the air. Each soldier seemed stiffer than before. None of them looked at the three boys or did anything except stare in the same direction. No one spoke or made any sound.

Every soldier was present except Gero. Footsteps could be heard down the hallway. Gero appeared. Seconds later, he was followed by the innkeeper. The innkeeper wasn't dressed properly. He wore a long nightshirt and looked as if he had been dragged from bed.

"I'll go get the horses," he said, a yawn escaping at the end of the sentence. He disappeared out the front door. While he was gone, they all made their way outside to wait for the keeper to return. A few minutes later, he returned with four horses. It took a couple of trips, but eventually he had brought around all of them.

"Hope your stay was pleasant," the keeper scoffed and walked inside.

Gero, clearly distracted, didn't even notice the keeper's tone. Llider knew at this point something was wrong because normally the keeper would have a black eye with a tone like that.

"We're leaving now. We are not stopping until I say. No complaints, no questions." He mounted his horse and jammed his heels, sending his horse forward. Everyone else followed suit, and they raced out of town. Gero didn't slow down once they cleared the gate. In fact, they sped up. They had never traveled this fast, but for some reason Gero had led them away from the town rather hastily. Once the town of Dagmar was just a dark spot on the horizon, Gero slowed up a little, resuming his original pace. The soldiers seemed to relax, and the tension disappeared.

They traveled a lot that day, and an eerie silence could be felt through the group. They were about six days from the castle. They were about to connect with the road that traveled south. It marked the official six-day ride to the castle.

That night, they camped off the main road. Although the tension was gone, Gero definitely seemed more alert. The next morning, the sky had darkened and rain had started to fall, making their progress slower. Although it kept them cool through the day, it drenched their clothes. When the night came, the rain had increased and was pounding down on them. Lightning streaked the sky, followed by thunder, which caused the ground beneath them to shake.

"We're going to camp under those trees," Gero yelled over the rain. He was pointing at the forest a little ways off the main road. He led the group to the trees. It didn't help much, but it was better than nothing.

The soldiers all hunkered down, using miscellaneous items to shield themselves from the rain. Some used blankets. Others tried to position themselves under their horses, which didn't work well. Others just suffered through it. Gero seemed to have disappeared completely.

"What do we do now?" Llider yelled over the rain.

"Well, doesn't look like this is going anywhere anytime soon. We might as well make the best of it," Oli replied. Heruki was crouched beside them, hugging himself, trying to keep warm.

"Let's try to find something to build a shelter with," Llider said as he grabbed some blankets he had. They were soaked though, and water just poured through them. Heruki tried some big leaves he had found, but it did no good as water flowed around them. Nothing seemed to work. The rain was too hard, and the wind wasn't letting up. Realizing they were just going to have to suffer, they sat huddled together, trying to maintain some of the warmth.

"So, what now?" Llider laughed slightly. "This is ridiculous."

"Well, I don't know about you, but I'm not going to be able to sleep with this. How about you guys?" Oli replied.

Both shook their heads. "How about we—" He was cut off by a flash of lightning just on the edge of the forest, and a dark shape became visible.

"What was that?" Heruki yelled, both Llider and Oli having seen the same thing.

"It looked like someone on horseback," Llider said, his voice shaky. A mix of cold, fear and nervousness took his voice over. There was another flash of lightning, illuminating the shape again, this time a little farther away. It was definitely someone on horseback. "Let's go," Llider said, his legs protesting the sudden movement.

The storm seemed to pick up as they made their way out of the forest. The wind was violently moving the trees. Groans could be heard from them as they resisted the wind, trying not to break. The rain pounded on every surface it found, making it almost impossible for them to see. The only light was the constant lightning. When they exited the forest, the rain seemed to lighten up slightly in front of them. The main road was only a few hundred feet away.

Llider looked behind him, and the storm seemed to be stronger. He couldn't even see the soldiers anymore, even though they couldn't be that far away.

"Where'd he go?" Heruki said. With that, another lightning bolt erupted, illuminating two shapes.

"Look!" Llider pointed towards the road just as it went dark again. "There's two of them now."

They were seated on horses. No features could be seen, just dark silhouettes. Another lightning bolt shot across the sky. This time Llider got a better look and could tell that the two were staring directly in his direction. Llider's heart stopped as fear struck him. Another bolt illuminated the shadows again.

"We need to get back!" He heard Oli yelling, pulling on Llider.

But he couldn't move or break his stare. He seemed transfixed. Oli's words seemed miles away. When the light faded, the eyes of the shadow started to glow, piercing the darkness. Instantly, Llider fell to his knees, his muscles giving out and his vision blurring. A scream pierced through the air. *Was that me?* Llider thought. It must have been because pain pulsed through his body. Oli and Heruki, on reaction alone, grabbed him so he didn't collapse to the ground. Llider raised one hand and pointed to the location of the two shadows as his vision faded and he fell unconscious.

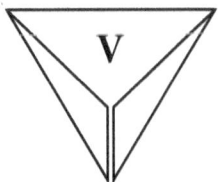

V

Llider awoke, not sure where he was. His body didn't hurt anymore. He was lying on his back, looking up at a clear sky. Fluffy clouds floated lazily, casting small shadows around him. He stood up and looked around. He was standing exactly where he had fallen. Green grass surrounded him, the smell of dew in the air. The forest was glistening from the previous rainfall. Remembering a little of what happened, Llider looked at the road where the shadows had been. No one was there. Heruki and Oli were also nowhere to be found.

He looked left and right and found no one.

"HELLO?" he screamed. No answer. He ran back to the camp where all the soldiers had been. Gone. There was no sign that they had even been there. The rain must have washed everything away. He ran back out of the forest and stood there trying to figure out what happened and where everyone was. Nothing. This didn't make any sense. Why was he left? Then he heard it—a horse.

He looked down the road as a silhouette formed. The silhouette was similar to the shadows he had seen the previous night. This person also sat upon a horse.

Llider. A voice entered his head, and he panicked. He crouched down as his eyes scanned around him, looking for threats.

Llider. He heard it again and realized it was coming from the silhouette on the horse. *You must find truth. Do not fall for the false pretense of this life. If you are curious, seek me out. My name is Salvator. I live in a city filled with life, inhabited by people who know. Seek me out, and all shall be understood.*

"What? That makes no sense," Llider called out, but the silhouette was already gone. The sky began to get brighter and brighter until Llider had to shield his eyes from the blinding light. Rain started to hit his face, and he felt the hard ground under his back again. He also heard the voices of Oli and Heruki. They were calling to him. He opened his eyes to find Oli's and Heruki's faces looking down on him. Rain still poured from the sky. He tried to move, but his body was still stiff.

"Llider! You're alive. What happened? One minute you were screaming, the next you were unconscious," Oli said, his voice filled with concern.

"I don't know," Llider said as he tried to remember, things still a little hazy. He shot up, looking at the road. The silhouettes were gone.

"What is it?" Oli asked, nervously looking where Llider was staring.

"Did you see the shadows?" Llider asked, breathing heavily. "They were standing over there. There were two of them, and then their eyes started glowing. Did you see them?"

"Their eyes?" Heruki replied, confused. "We saw the silhouettes, but as soon as you fainted, we got distracted and they disappeared."

"Are you sure you're okay?" Oli said, concern filling his voice and eyes. "Let's get you back to camp, the sun should be coming up soon."

The rain lessened as they returned back to camp. It was manageable now. Once they were back and all huddled close, Oli looked at Llider. "Okay, clearly we missed something. What happened?"

Llider spent the next several minutes recounting what had happened. Neither Oli nor Heruki said anything through the entire story. At the mention of Salvator though, Llider noticed, they did steal a glance at each other.

"So you guys didn't see anything?" Llider said after he finished. The other two shook their heads.

"We were both standing there trying to see the silhouettes better when you started screaming and collapsed. We caught you but had to lay you down because you were out. We tried to wake you, but it didn't work. Then you woke up by yourself." Oli recounted. "By the time you woke up, the silhouettes were gone. You were only out a few seconds."

"Only a few seconds," Llider said, shocked. "It seemed like hours." There was no reply for a moment as the three resided into their own thoughts.

"Let's think this over and talk about it more tomorrow. We need to get some rest," Heruki finally said. "It's probably not smart to say anything to anyone else either." They all agreed and closed their eyes. Llider sat there for what seemed like hours with his eyes closed, replaying the dream over and over.

He didn't know when he fell asleep or for how long, but was woken by the sound of the soldiers moving around him. The rain had stopped, and the sun had appeared from behind the clouds. Rays of heat were breaking through the tops of the trees. The heat felt good on Llider's face. The soldiers were already up and ready.

Expecting Gero to come reprimand them any second, Llider and his friends got up and readied their horses.

"Let's go! We have a lot of time to make up." Gero appeared, no evidence he had been caught in a storm. He wasn't wet at all. He looked like he had slept inside all night. Llider looked at him and the other soldiers. Definitely a difference. Gero mounted his horse without a second glance and lead everyone out of the forest and back on the road.

The road was muddy, which made for a noisy ride. Way different than the drowning silence that normally followed their group. Llider was extremely tired since he hadn't slept, and Heruki and Oli looked like zombies. Most of the day, they didn't talk, and if they did, it was very minimal. It was just too much effort.

They traveled for two more days, finally reaching the fork. It hadn't rained again, and all of their clothes had been able to dry. Each night, Llider kept an alert eye while he slept, waking any time there was an odd noise. He had not forgotten about that night and continued to assess the whole thing, trying to figure out the meaning.

He had never heard of Salvator, and he wondered what the hell a "city filled with life, inhabited by people who know" meant. He had no clue, and no matter how he put it, it didn't make sense.

On the fourth day, they passed the road leading to Mesta. Mesta was a very small town, more of a trading post. Ziveer, the southern city, used Mesta for this purpose. The plan had been to stop there, but Gero seemed to be in a hurry to make it to the castle.

Llider sat atop Sage as she walked along. It was mid-afternoon, another day of travel after not sleeping for almost three days. Every night, Llider would lie awake, any noise making him shift his attention. This happened every night since the incident.

Llider was lazily looking around as the unit walked in formation. He was half asleep.

"HALT!" Gero shouted, his attention focused on the path ahead. Every solider went rigid. This knocked Llider out of his daze. In front of them, blocking the road, stood four cloaked men. They sat atop great white steeds. Their faces were concealed beneath their hoods. Llider recognized them from the tavern. He looked at Heruki and Oli, and they nodded, letting Llider know that they recognized them also. Two of them were holding bows. The other two were resting their hands on the pommel of their swords. Their bows were unique—more art than weapons for killing. They definitely weren't man-made.

"In the name of the king, remove yourself from our path now," Gero commanded, a hint of threat in his voice. No answer. Gero placed his hand on his hilt, the soldiers following suit. Again, Llider noticed how the soldiers did everything in unison.

After a few minutes of silence, an unknown language came from one of the cloaked figures, "Cwellan se soldarius!" Three more hoods appeared on each side of the road, each with arrows already notched in their bows. Arrows suddenly flew through the air, killing a few of the soldiers, some being blocked.

"It's the Drutas! Kill them!" Gero commanded, dodging one of the arrows. The soldiers all drew their swords and attacked. The four original Drutas had let their hoods fall, revealing their Elven features.

In the commotion, Llider looked around and noticed the majority were Elves, some human. The four main Elves had cut through three soldiers and were already engaged with more. Gero himself had taken out four of the Drutas, leaving only six left.

The Drutas were far more skilled than the soldiers. Most of the time, it was two, sometimes three, soldiers to a Drutan. Despite the box the soldiers had created around the three boys, Llider and the other two drew their weapons, ready to help. Each time a Drutan would come near them, he would get engaged with another soldier, almost to a point that it seemed the Drutas were trying to avoid them.

In the end, nine soldiers, including Gero, remained. All of the Drutas had fallen. There were dead bodies everywhere, and blood stained the swords of every living soldier. Gero had been wounded, evidenced by blood running down his hand.

Gero looked over the scene. "We're leaving now. We're going to ride straight, not stopping until we reach the castle walls. Understood?"

"Sir!" the soldiers responded. There was no care of the fallen, not so much as a glance at them, and they were riding again, this time pushing their horses to their limits.

A couple of hours later, they came to a small stream where they stopped for a break. It seemed Gero stopped mainly for the horses.

"Who are the Drutas?" Llider quietly asked the other two, making sure no one else heard him.

Heruki shrugged, but Oli answered, "You two have never heard of the Drutas?" Both shook their heads. Oli sighed. "I can't believe you never heard the stories. The Drutas are a group of rebels who appeared when the Thirteen Chosen disappeared. The land started to fall apart again, wars breaking out, and the Capitol tried to put order back in. The Drutas have been terrorizing the king's attempts to bring peace throughout, or so we're told. There are many different stories going around. Some say the Drutas are good, led by the Thirteenth Chosen, but the majority agree they're trying to overthrow the Capitol and take over."

Llider let everything sink in for a little. This was the first he had heard about the Drutas. He then asked, "So the Drutas have Elves? From what I know of Elves, they tend to stick to their own land. They don't really mess with the problems of man."

Oli sighed, "Man, I know about as much as you do now. We just need to keep our eyes open now. We may not be so lucky next time."

"Time to go!" Gero yelled out. With that, they mounted their horses and continued their very hurried pace.

About two hours later, the castle walls came into view. Llider had never seen something so large. They were thousands of feet high, or so they seemed. The top of the wall was outlined in crenellations, allowing for good defensive positioning. A single drawbridge lay open with soldiers lining the entrance, creating a single path into the castle.

"Get into formation, the three boys in the middle," Gero commanded as they neared the entrance. The soldiers immediately shifted to form rows of two, Gero leading and the three boys together in the middle.

As they neared the gate, Llider could make out guards patrolling the parapet on top of the wall. They passed the line of soldiers, none of which glanced at them. They just blankly looked forward.

Inside the outer ward, people were everywhere. They stopped to watch the battered group walk through the city. Opar'Leet was the biggest city Llider had ever seen. Houses and stores were all around. A little ways to the left sat the keep. It towered above the rest of the town, giving a clear view of everything around.

People crowded the streets, running from shop to shop. As the unit made their way down the street, people would stop to stare at the three boys. They were used to the soldiers, but these were new recruits, and everyone wanted to get a look.

Gero led them north through the city. They turned left and made their way to an area with more open ground. A huge structure towered behind the training grounds. Hundreds of soldiers were practicing their swordsmanship, their archery and many other skills. They made their way to the front of the building past the training grounds where they dismounted their horses, tied them up, and grabbed their belongings.

"Stay here," Gero commanded to his soldiers and then turned to address the three. "This is the barracks. It's where you'll train and live. I'm going to show you who will be your trainer," Gero stated as he led them into the barracks.

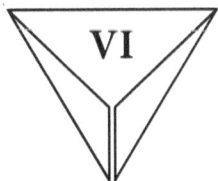

VI

The main hall was very plain. There were two doors on either side of the hall. Directly in front of the main door was a desk set up a little off the wall, just enough for someone to sit behind it. Behind the desk sat a portly, unofficial looking man. He wore plain black pants and a plain white shirt. A sword hung at his waist. He glanced at them dully as they entered. He had the same expressionless look as all the other soldiers. At the sight of Gero, he got up and walked around the desk.

He shook Gero's hand, "Welcome, Gero, you're back early."

"We made good time," Gero answered quickly, not wanting to get into any more detail. "Here are the three new recruits. Can I be done with them already?"

"Yes, yes. One moment." The portly fellow turned and grabbed a few pieces of paper and handed them to Gero. Gero took them, turned and walked out. "He's always been quite a talker that one," the portly fellow mused. He turned to the three. "I'm Rueben. I keep the barracks organized and make sure the new recruits are settled. Right, now let me show you to your room."

He turned to his left and walked through the door, leading the three boys. They immediately went up a set of stairs and turned left again. This led to a long hallway. The hallway had many doors on each side, all marked with a number. There were so many doors. It was clearly the berthing. They walked for about five minutes until Rueben stopped and turned to a door on their left. It had the number forty-five on it.

"Here's the room you three will stay in." He opened the door to reveal very small quarters. Against each of the walls were beds. There were no windows, and the only place to put one's belongings was under the beds. "Are you three hungry?"

They shook their heads. They were too wound up to be hungry.

"Ok, go to bed then. It's late, so get some rest. Someone will come get you tomorrow to orient you to everything. Pay attention because you will only be told once. Your training will start the following day." He then left, leaving the boys to fill in all the blanks.

"Well, this is lovely. I see we got the king's suite," Llider said sarcastically. The other two chuckled as they made their way into the room. They chose their beds and tossed their stuff under.

"So what do you think is next for us?" Oli asked.

"I'm not sure. I guess we'll find out tomorrow," Llider replied, his thoughts drifting to Mirafol. He missed his comfortable bed in his warm house. He missed the smell of bacon cooking in the morning. Things had changed drastically since his simple life in Mirafol. He wondered if anything would ever be the same. The last thing he remembered before he dozed off was the soft, held-back sobs he heard from Heruki.

Llider woke to a loud pounding on the door. Rubbing his eyes, he got out of bed and opened the door. A short man stood in the doorway. He wore beige pants with a matching leather vest covering a white shirt. His face was rounded, and he had a nose that shot out from the middle of his face.

"Get ready," he said. His voice was very deep. Llider nodded and closed the door. He turned around to see Oli and Heruki sitting up in their beds, both with blank expressions on their faces from having just woken up.

"Time to go, I guess," Llider said, and they all threw on their gear. The man was standing right outside the door waiting as they walked out. He motioned for them to follow him and started walking back to the main hall. The three followed.

"My name is Ulti. I'll be showing you where you eat, the areas you train and what weapons you use. I will also show you where to wash up." Ulti opened the door to the main hall.

"This is the main entrance. Behind us, where we came from, is the housing." He crossed the hall and entered the room directly across from the berthing door. This one was completely different. It was a huge room, and there were tables that crossed the length of the room.

"This is the mess hall. This is where you'll eat." Hundreds of soldiers sat eating. Ulti led them to a table which had plates on it filled with small portions of food. They each grabbed one and sat down. The food wasn't fresh at all. It was a few pieces of bacon, which were cold, a couple of eggs, which were soggy, and some slop that tasted like grits, but Llider wasn't sure.

Llider started to eat. Realizing how hungry he was, he slammed the food down his throat, and before he knew it, it was all gone. He sat back with a sigh. "Wow, I didn't realize how hungry I was."

"Yeah … tell … me … about it," Oli said with a mouthful, bits of food spraying out of his mouth. Heruki just nodded enthusiastically, unable to speak with the amount of food he was trying to put in his.

They all finished eating and sat back with a great sigh of relief, their stomachs now full. Ulti returned a few minutes later.

"Okay good, you're all done. Follow me." He led them back out the door they had come in and through another door, which led outside. The sun was beating down on them. It seemed hotter than usual.

"Here are the main training grounds," Ulti said, casting his hand out. Soldiers were already on the field. Some were sparring with swords while others shot arrows at targets, some moving and others stationary. On another field, there were soldiers practicing different formations, offensive and defensive. The soldiers here were fighting perfectly. Their faces were expressionless, and their attacks seemed effortless. The men practicing the formations, Llider noticed, didn't make one mistake. They were perfect. After seeing all of the different areas in this field, they went back to the mess hall for a meal break.

When they were done, Ulti led them around the main training grounds to the location where they were going to begin their training.

"This is the new recruits field," Ulti told them. This field was much smaller than the others, but there were also a lot less soldiers on it—Llider estimated about fifty. The recruits were only practicing sword and bow, nothing else. They sparred with each other and shot at stationary targets. The soldiers here were very sloppy and not precise at all. When they were sparring, you could see the effort in their faces.

"Most of the recruits are only here a few weeks. We generally recruit more experienced fighters. This is more of a testing ground to see where you need improvement. If you're good enough, you move up quickly. If not, well, you stay here for a while."

Once they left the new recruits field, they were walking back to the barracks when Llider noticed a small building on the opposite side of the training grounds. Soldiers were standing in a line that started from the main door.

"What's that building over there?" Llider asked Ulti.

Ulti looked at the building. "That's special training you receive once you finish your new recruit stage." Llider stared at it feeling very curious. If it made him as perfect as the other soldiers, he wanted it immediately.

"Last but not least, the bathhouse. This is a public bathing area. Anyone at any time can use it. It's always open." Ulti showed them inside. It was a small building behind the barracks.

The day had gone by already, and the sun was getting low in the sky as they made their way back to the mess hall for supper.

"What's the special training?" Llider asked Ulti as they walked back.

"I guess you'll just have to wait and see," Ulti smiled slyly.

"You," Llider pressed, "seem different. A lot of the soldiers seem much more serious."

Ulti chuckled, actually chuckled. Llider hadn't heard a response like that from a soldier in quite some time. "I am," was all he said in a tone that meant the conversation was over.

"So listen," Ulti began as they sat at their table for

dinner, "your commander will get you in the morning. Be ready by dawn. You can find your way back to your room, yeah?" They nodded, and Ulti left.

"So what do you think the special training is?" Llider asked the other two immediately after Ulti left, his excitement clearly pouring out.

"Probably magic training," Heruki replied just as enthusiastically.

"It did seem weird that there was such a big line," Llider interjected. "Shouldn't special training be done together?"

"Maybe it's done by a single mage," Heruki nudged, still liking the idea that it was magic.

"We can keep guessing or," Oli's voice was soft, "we can just get through the recruiting stage quickly like we know we are." This put a damper on the excitement as he went back to eating. Llider wasn't going to let this dampen his excitement. He just didn't continue talking and kept it to himself.

Later that night, they had made it back to their rooms and settled in. Llider lay there staring up at the ceiling, his mind racing. Sleep was finally able to overcome him, and it took him to an entirely different world.

He was walking through the training fields towards the special training building. There was no line this time, so he walked right in. It was smaller than he expected inside—big enough to hold maybe fifteen people. Sure enough, there were about ten people standing in a large circle. They were all facing the center of the circle, hands in front of them. A white light was glowing from their hands.

"What's going on?" Llider asked quietly, almost as if he was hoping they wouldn't hear him. Every single person turned their head to look straight at Llider. Their

eyes were not eyes but glowing white. They all turned and raised their hands at Llider. A huge blinding light flashed, sending energy at him.

Instinctively, he raised his hands and turned his head. He felt a burning in his hands. Not painful, just warm. He opened his eyes to see a huge wall of fire before him, blocking the white light on the other side. He realized the fire was emanating from his palms, the heat spreading all over his body. The intensity became too much, and Llider fell over, hitting his head and blacking out.

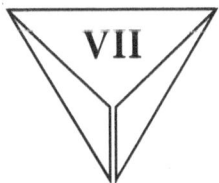

VII

Llider shot up in bed, sweat beading down his forehead. He wiped the sweat from his brow as he saw Oli sit up and look around blankly. With a very tired voice, he asked, "Is it hot in here?" and threw his blanket off of him and lay back down.

Llider was unsure whether or not Oli had actually woken up or if he was just talking in his sleep. Either way, he was sleeping again. Llider threw his legs off his bed and touched the floor with his feet. Right away, he pulled them up, noticing how cold the floor was. He could swear he even heard a sizzle. He gingerly tested the ground until he could comfortably put his feet down flat. The coolness of the floor seemed to spread through his entire body, and he sighed with relief. After he had cooled off a little, he allowed himself to lie back down in his bed and fell back asleep.

The next morning, they were roused by a quick knock as the door swung open. Ulti stood there. "Get up, your training begins today," he said with a deadpan look.

"Good morning to you too, Ulti," Heruki replied, rubbing sleep out of his eyes.

"Did I say speak, boy?" Ulti turned to look at Heruki. "Get your ass out of bed and follow me now." His face had turned redder, but he remained expressionless.

Confused by the sudden change in Ulti, the three got ready in no time. They followed Ulti to the mess hall where he stood and watched them eat with his arms crossed.

"Are you okay?" Llider asked Ulti after a few minutes. He didn't respond, just kept looking straight. When they had finished eating, he told them to follow him and led them to the training grounds.

"Here are the new recruits for you. They've been informed of everything and will start their training today," Ulti said plainly.

"Good, I've been expecting them!" the soldier said sternly and turned his attention to the three. Ulti turned and left. "My name is Kilas. But you will refer to me as 'Sir' whenever you address me. You three will train separately." Kilas called over two other soldiers who had been observing the other recruits. "This is Yasha and this is Rakai." He motioned to them as he introduced them. "Heruki and Oli will go with them. They will train you two. Llider, you will train with me."

Heruki and Oli nodded to Llider and left with the other soldiers. Kilas turned to Llider, "Now, let's see what league you're in. Draw your sword. Well, swords," he said, noticing Llider carried two. "First, are you skilled with those?" he asked as Llider drew them.

"My father trained me. He was a sword fighter a long time ago. So I'm pretty good," Llider said proudly.

"Okay, good. Then you should get through training quickly. Let's begin."

Kilas was a very interesting character. He was a shorter man—a little shorter than Llider. His build was bigger though. He had a moustache that curved around his lips and formed a goatee. His eyes were dark; they resembled black holes, as he didn't seem to have any pupils. His hair, although black and very visible, was extremely short. His sword was much different than any other; it was a short blade that curved backwards.

Kilas stood with no expression on his face. His stare seemed to pierce Llider's soul, and Llider flinched, not able to stare back. He instantly regretted this as Kilas lunged forward, striking him with the side of his sword on his left arm. Llider dropped to one knee, unable to hold himself up from the blow.

His arm throbbed, and he realized he had underestimated Kilas. He was much faster than Llider had thought. Kilas' expression did not change as he took his fighting stance once more. Llider slowly stood up and got back into his stance, his shoulder still throbbing. He focused his mind on Kilas, not faulting this time. For the next few minutes, the two stood waiting for the other to flinch. Neither moved nor blinked. Llider's arm started to shake, the soreness from the blow spreading. Finally, Llider couldn't take it anymore and charged at Kilas, his one sword going directly at his stomach. Kilas used his sword to easily deflect it. Llider brought his other sword around to try to strike Kilas. Kilas moved with extraordinary speed and dodged it. Kilas, using Llider's momentum to his advantage, threw Llider off balance and to the ground. Llider swirled around on his knees to prepare for a blow, but none came. Kilas stood looking at Llider and, in one motion, sheathed his sword.

"Well, you have potential but definitely need work," Kilas stated. "By the time I'm done with you, you'll be of good use to us. Let's go again." They sparred back and forth the rest of the day, only taking a break to eat. Kilas didn't eat with Llider, and Llider also didn't see Heruki or Oli. After mealtime, they continued to spar, Kilas teaching different moves as they went until it was time for supper.

"That's it for today," Kilas said as he sheathed his sword. "We'll continue tomorrow. Meet me here in the morning." With that, he made his departure.

For the next couple of weeks, Llider and Kilas trained. Llider didn't see Heruki or Oli at all. They had been moved to another room. Kilas taught Llider many skills. Every day, they ran different exercises including running every morning for twenty miles. Llider was given weighted ankle and wrist straps to wear nonstop, which, to his resentment, were increased in weight every few days. He was required to wear them at all times, even when sleeping.

After a couple months of training, Llider had become faster, stronger and even a challenge for Kilas. Llider awoke one morning and did his normal routine. He got ready, ate, and found Kilas standing at the top of the training grounds. Something was different today. Kilas was not in his usual training clothes. He was wearing his normal trousers and a plain white shirt, the kind usually worn under armor. His sword was sheathed at his side, and his hand rested atop the pommel. Llider walked up to him.

"Morning, Sir," Llider greeted him.

Kilas nodded in return. "Llider, you have trained well. You have increased in strength, size and ability. Your sword skill has become extremely impressive. Your bow skills are as sharp as ever. You may now remove the weights on your legs and arms." Llider gladly slid the weights off his arms and legs, the lighter skin seeing sun for the first time in a while. Feeling relief, he realized how much lighter his whole body was. He jabbed the air a few times. He was astounded at how quick he was. It was like having a whole new body. He felt as light as a feather.

"So," Kilas continued, "I am your final test. If you can defeat me in a sword fight, you will leave the recruits and join the main army. This will not be like when we spar. This will be full speed and with no mercy. Are you ready for that?"

"Sir!" Llider responded. He felt invincible. He was ready.

"Good. First one to draw blood from the chest wins. Remove your armor." Kilas removed his white shirt, revealing his bare chest, his muscles rippling in the sun. Llider did the same. They stood, swords drawn, facing each other. Silence enveloped them as they focused on each other. Kilas broke the silence, lunging at Llider. Llider sidestepped and blocked. He countered with a strike at Kilas' back. Kilas twisted and deflected his attack, knocking Llider's sword away. Kilas returned, thrusting at Llider and, before he was blocked, spun to the right side and jabbed again. Llider barely moved out of the way but kept his footing. With a series of fancy sword movements, he was able to knock Kilas' sword out of his hand. While undefended, Llider struck. Kilas lunged forward, grabbing Llider's wrist and spun around, Llider's blade drawing blood from Kilas' wrist. Kilas jumped back, and before Llider could strike again, he recovered his sword. Kilas lunged forward and, making contact with one of Llider's swords, was able to slide his own down the blade and cut Llider's hand. One of Llider's swords fell from his hand and landed on the ground. Llider spun around, separating himself from Kilas.

His frustration grew as he was having more trouble than he expected. He stood staring at Kilas. His arm began to throb, and he remembered his first fight with

Kilas. He had been struck in his arm, but he thought the wound had healed. Llider guessed it had been aggravated again. Kilas glanced at Llider's arm—a mistake.

Llider immediately lunged with intense speed. He spun his sword in his hand and very quickly brought it down. Kilas barely blocked. Keeping up the momentum, Llider spun his sword around, causing Kilas' sword to follow, and with a few movements, he relieved Kilas of his sword. Llider ran his blade across Kilas' chest. A faint line of blood appeared, announcing Llider's victory.

Llider stood silent as he caught his breath. He didn't say anything, just observed Kilas. Kilas continued to stare back at Llider. His chest moving up and down with every breath. A few seconds went by as Kilas seemed to refocus on Llider.

"Congratulations," he said. Llider could see his eyes shifting. Something had spooked him, it seemed. "You have defeated me. That is a huge accomplishment." He continued in a hurried voice. "I...," he looked down the field a little, "I must go. I'll send someone for you later." Before Llider could respond, Kilas had grabbed up his shirt and departed.

Stunned at being left so suddenly, Llider stood watching as Kilas disappeared. Uncertain on what to do, he decided to go to the mess hall. The sun was almost at its highest point in the sky, and his empty stomach was making noises. Some soldiers were already eating. He grabbed a plate and scarfed down the food.

Not knowing what to do, he decided to wander a little. He made his way back to the recruits' field, hoping he could find Heruki or Oli. He made his way around a few of the fields but found nothing, just soldiers he didn't recognize. Defeated, he decided to head back to the barracks.

"Llider!" he heard his name yelled frantically. He turned to see Oli and Heruki running up to him, their faces red. "We … need … to … talk…," Oli said between deep breaths. "Follow us! Now!" Oli was running again, Heruki close behind him. They led him into the barracks through a door that Llider had never noticed before.

The doorway led to a new hallway. The path sloped down, going underground. It wasn't long before they came to a door and entered it. Oli stood at the doorway and, when they were all in, looked out, making sure no one had followed, and closed the door.

"What the hell, guys? What's going on?" Llider said impatiently.

"Just a moment," Oli hushed him. They sat quietly, nothing but silence was heard. While he sat, Llider noticed that Heruki and Oli had changed quite a lot. Heruki no longer had the soft face of a sixteen year old. His face had aged, not really with time, but experience. His body was much larger, and he had muscles poking out where they weren't before. Oli had also changed quite a lot. His features were more defined. He seemed to be nothing but solid muscle now, and his hair was the biggest difference. It had been cut short.

"Okay," Oli finally broke the silence, "we're alone. I just wanted to make sure we weren't followed."

"Followed? What's going on you guys?" Llider said, losing his patience.

"We found something out," Oli started speaking very quickly. "We have to tell you. Remember how we thought something weird was going on with the soldiers?" Llider nodded eagerly. "Well, Heruki and I were heading back to the barracks one night. We were passing the special train-ings building, and we got curious. We decided to go check things out. We walked up to the entrance, as there wasn't a line. There were two guards. They stopped us and sent us away. Heruki," he nodded at him, "had the bright idea to climb to the top." He paused, taking a longer breath.

"So we snuck up to the top. It wasn't too hard to climb," Heruki continued as Oli caught his breath. "At the top was an opening with some light shining out of it. We went over to look in and we saw ... what they were doing. There was a guy lying on the table writhing. A cloaked man sat near the guy's head, leaning over him. His hands were—"

The door flew open, and they all jumped. Four guards stood there. "What are you doing in here! You're not allowed in here." The guards reached forward, grabbing the three. As one, they pushed back, knocking the guards away. They tried to get free, but the four guards overpowered them.

The three were led out of the room, the guards right on their heels. They were led back upstairs but not to their quarters. They were placed in three separate rooms. These rooms were definitely different—more like cells than lodgings. The doors were locked from the outside, and there was nothing on the inside, just a bare floor and walls. Llider could hear the soldiers throwing Heruki and Oli in the rooms next to him.

"You three stay here and guard the doors. I'll go get Kilas." Footsteps could be heard leaving the hallway.

"What's going on?" Llider yelled at the guards. The door swung open as the guard stormed in and hit Llider across his face, knocking him to the floor.

"No talking. Got it? Kilas will decide what to do with you." The guard exited, closing the door with a bang. Llider sat there silently, minutes turning into what seemed like hours. He could hear the constant shuffles of feet from one of the other two.

After what seemed like ages, footsteps were heard coming closer. Llider perked up when he heard voices. He couldn't make out what was being said; they were too quiet. A door opened, and he heard what sounded like someone punching something, and then the sound of dragging. The door closed.

"Heruki! Oli!" he yelled. The guard's face appeared in the only opening the door had.

"Do you want me to come in there again?" he threatened. "Say one more thing, and you'll wish you were dead."

Llider went silent. Another unknown amount of time went by when more footsteps were heard. Again, voices. "… needs to go straight there. No stops," he heard. Confused, he scooted closer to the door, trying to hear more. "If someone asks," that sounded like Kilas, Llider thought, "tell them it's on my orders." Footsteps again. Llider scooted back. Another door opened. Again, it sounded like someone was punched, and then more dragging. Silence.

What is happening? Llider thought. He finished his training, and now he was in a cell. This wasn't right. Time slipped by, no sun to tell what time it was or even if it was still daylight. His mind wandered, and at one point he wasn't sure if he was sleeping or not.

"He's too important," voices in his head said. Was that in his head? He wasn't sure. "He can't find out." Those were definitely voices, but real or not? His head was groggy, his stomach empty, and he felt like he had paper in his mouth.

The truth, find the truth.

He definitely heard that. His eyes shot open, and he looked around. No one. He realized it was all in his head after all. He closed his eyes and focused, trying to hear it again. Nothing. Silence again. He thought it had said, "The truth, find the truth." He had no clue what that meant.

Again, time seemed to slip by until he finally heard footsteps once more. He pushed himself up against a wall so he was upright. The door opened.

Kilas stood there, concern on his face. "What have they done to you?" He walked in and helped Llider to his feet. Llider threw his arm over Kilas' shoulders, using him for support. "I can't believe they threw you in here. What a huge mistake. Someone will answer for this." His voice was soft with an edge of something else underneath. Kilas helped him out of the cell. The guards were all gone. The hall was empty.

"Where," Llider coughed, "are the guards?" Llider's throat burned with thirst. Kilas set Llider down on one of the chairs.

"Mert!" Kilas yelled. A recruit, Llider could tell by what he was wearing, walked in. "Get Llider some water right away." Mert turned and ran out. "As soon as I heard about what happened, I sent the guards away."

"Heruki … Oli.…" More coughs.

"They're fine. They were released earlier. I wanted to come get you myself." Mert returned with water and handed it to Llider. He grabbed it and chugged it down. "Whoa, slow down," Kilas said as Llider drained the cup. "Well, Mert, I think some more is needed." Mert took the cup and ran out again. "So, why did they throw you in the cell?"

"I don't know. We were in this small room behind

the main hall, and...," he paused looking at Kilas. His face was soft and friendly but there was something else in his eyes. He decided against telling him the story Oli and Heruki had started to tell him. "We were just exploring, and I guess we found ourselves in a place we weren't allowed to go."

"Ah ha," Kilas said. "That's all?" Llider nodded. "Well that's unfortunate. Rest assured, those guards will be punished for their damages." Kilas smiled. Mert had returned with a new glass of water, and Llider downed it again. "Think you're up for your special training? I know you must be tired, but you have to be excited."

Llider thought for a moment. Something was off, but he thought best to go along with it. "Yeah, I guess so."

They left the room and out of the barracks, Mert close behind. The sun was rising. He had been in that room for almost a day.

"Are you okay to go from here?" Kilas turned and looked at Llider.

"Yeah, I think so." Llider just wanted to get away from everyone and collect his thoughts. This was perfect.

"Okay good. Mert is receiving his special training today too, so he'll go with you. Be quick though; they're expecting you. To make up for the mistake, I made sure they'll put you in front of the line as soon as you show up."

Damn, Llider thought. "Okay, we'll head right there," Llider said, trying to fake enthusiasm. Kilas smiled, clearly waiting for them to leave. Mert and Llider started towards the training building.

On their way there, Mert was nonstop. He kept talking and talking about how excited he was. Llider, lost in his own thoughts, just kept absently acknowledging

71

him. As they neared the building, Llider turned to Mert. "I forgot something back in the barracks. Go on without me. I won't be long." Mert started to protest, but Llider was already running back.

When he was far enough that no one was paying attention, he doubled back and sneaked around the side of the building. It was time to figure out what was going on in this place.

He snuck to the back of the building and found a way to scale the wall. He climbed to the top and onto the roof. Sure enough, there was an opening in the roof. He walked over to it and looked in. Llider went pale. What he saw was appalling. There, strapped down on the table, was Mert.

Hovering over his head was a man in a white cloak. His hands were placed about two inches away from either side of Mert's temples. White energy was surging out of each hand and into Mert's head. Mert's body convulsed, and he strained against the straps holding him. His veins looked as they were threatening to burst. His face contorted in odd shapes, betraying the pain in his body. In his mouth was a piece of wood held in by a strap. Llider couldn't take his eyes off of the sight.

Completely focused on what was happening, he jumped when he heard someone clear their throat behind him. He looked over his shoulder just in time to see a club bash his face, searing pain erupting through his body. All went black.

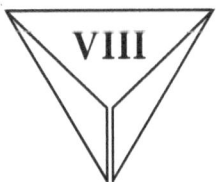

VIII

Azailia's body contorted as the wooden sword came in contact with her ribs. Her face was very sharp with very precise features. Her hair was golden blonde and very long. Her eyes were the color of the sea. She was thin but muscular. She had been training with her father, Harrus, since she was eight years old, but he could still best her. As she lay on the ground, her sword in her hand, she looked up and saw her father standing above her. His body cast an ominous shadow over her as the sun fell below the horizon.

"You're getting better," he said in a smooth voice. "I think you might be able to beat me soon." He offered his hand and helped her up.

The darkness surrounded them now as they stood apart. The only light available was the lamp hanging near the back door of the house.

"Remember, now that you can't see me well, rely on your senses over your sight." Her father lunged. Azailia's father taught her that the ability to fight at night was invaluable. To fight with one's senses other than sight could make them very dangerous. Therefore, every day for the past month, when the sun would disappear, they would train.

Azailia had still not mastered the skill, but she had fewer bruises than when they started. Her father had been training since he was a little boy and was very skilled. He had trained some of the best fighters around. In the beginning, she would rely on her eyes, but they would always deceive her. Even the shadows seemed to play against her. Over time, and after many sore nights, she learned to rely more on her senses. She learned to spread her attention around her until she was able to feel the movements of her father.

Her father deflected her jab, and she sensed him spin to the left. She turned and raised her sword just in time to block his attack. She pushed back, and just as she was about to strike, a blinding light flashed on the horizon followed by a loud boom. They both stopped and turned to look.

A huge orb erupted from the ground and curved up, rising high in the air. It continued to get brighter and brighter as it grew higher in the sky. The orb lit everything around as if the sun had risen again. It slowed down, and just before it stopped, it exploded, sending hundreds of streaking lights down to the Earth. It looked like fire raining from the sky.

"Follow me," her father commanded and raced inside. "Stay down here. I'll be right back." She sat down as Harrus disappeared upstairs. A few moments later, he returned, followed by her mother, Delia. They both wore black robes, which covered some light armor Azailia noticed. Their swords hung hidden at their sides.

"Where are you going?" Azailia said nervously.

"We'll be back. Your Mother and I are going to find out what happened," her father stated. "We'll be back soon. Stay inside and keep the door locked." And they left out the back door.

Azailia locked the door behind them and went to the window to just catch her parents racing off on horses towards the light. She watched until she could no longer see them.

The night seemed to stretch out, and she wasn't sure when she fell asleep, but she awoke as the sun fell over her face. She had fallen asleep on the small cushions that were positioned under the window. She looked outside and noticed that it was fairly early. The sun had just come up above the horizon.

Her parents still had yet to return. She tried to distract herself by making breakfast and then doing her chores. About midday, she was sweeping the porch in front of her house when she heard a lot of commotion coming from the center of town. It was unusual to hear so much noise, as her house was seated off from the main street. Curious about what was happening, she put the broom away, strapped her sword to her side and put her cloak on, covering her face.

A crowd of people gathered in the front of town. She moved through the crowd to get a clear view but not enough to stick out. A group of soldiers had ridden into town. They were fully armored and leading a carriage. They came to a stop in front of the crowd as they entered the town.

A man leaned out of the carriage and looked around over the people. He jumped off the step, brushed his pants and walked to the front, a pretentious smile on his face. He was very tall with extremely broad shoulders. He wore minimal armor. The way he held himself showed that he thought a bit too highly of himself.

"Where is the lord of this town?" he paused and then looked down at a piece of paper he held. "Reverus?"

A man pushed his way though the crowd to face the newcomer. "I am." He bowed. "Who might you be?"

"My name is Tracear," he responded, bowing back. "I was sent by the king to be your new envoy. I will act as your advisor. I am to help you and your people get what you need from the king." He turned his attention back to the carriage and clapped. The door swung open again. Another man exited the carriage.

This man was very different than anyone Azailia had ever seen. He had a very unique look. He wasn't ugly, but he wasn't attractive either. He had a very non-threatening face. His body was thin and very pale. He walked over to Tracear, looked at the crowd and smiled. His smile twisted up, causing a chill to shoot through Azailia's body. Her hand shot to the hilt of her sword.

His gaze moved through the crowd and landed on Azailia. They locked eyes for a moment. His eyes seemed to pierce through her soul, and she shook uncontrollably. After a moment, he continued his gaze of the crowd.

"Hello," the man spoke, his voice very raspy but smooth. "One of the requests Reverus had made a while ago was for a new Pravicus. For those who don't know the term, I am a doctor. However, I don't just treat physical injury. I can also help with mental stress. If you need anything, please come to me at any time." He bowed to the crowd. His moves were very calculated.

"Oh, thank you!" Reverus said cheerfully. "Let me show you where you'll stay and where the doctor can see patients. We just constructed a building in the center of the town. That should be perfect."

"You're too kind," the Pravicus said. "Since I just arrived, I will see everyone free of charge." People cheered at his statement. "Please make sure everyone knows. I will start tomorrow." They continued to talk as Reverus led them to the center of town. Most of the crowd followed, excited to see the new arrivals.

Azailia didn't move, she just stood, eyeing the newcomers. Something was off about these men; she just couldn't put her finger on it.

As the crowd moved away, Azailia turned to head back to her house. A friend of hers ran up.

"Aren't you excited?" Azailia's friend Rose said excitedly.

"Rose, did you notice anything unusual about this doctor?"

"Oh, come on, you're always suspicious. Can't we get one good thing?"

"I suppose … You didn't notice anything?"

"Well, besides the fact that he actually wants to help, I know, weird," she said sarcastically. "Come on, he seems like a good guy who's here to help."

"I hope you're right." Azailia forced a smile.

"That's the spirit! Now, I have to run home and get ready. I'll see you later!" And she ran off.

Azailia went back into her house. She hung her cloak up and removed her sword. Her thoughts went on to her parents who had still not returned. They had been gone for almost a day now. This was unlike them. She had started to worry again. She decided to distract herself with random chores around the house until it was late enough for her to go to sleep.

The next morning came suddenly. She washed, dressed and made breakfast. As she ate breakfast, she heard excited voices, once again coming from town. She threw on her cloak and grabbed her sword. She then made her way towards the center of town.

People were everywhere. They had all gotten up early so they could be the first to see the Pravicus. A stage had been erected on the side of the building. Instead of going into the crowd to wait, she moved around the crowd towards the back of town. She found the house she was looking for, and just before she was about to knock, she heard a crash inside. It sounded like something had fallen down. She decided against knocking and went around to the side of the house. She found a small hole that had been made for airflow and looked in to see a few soldiers holding Reverus down on the table.

The Pravicus was standing behind him by his head. He placed his hands on the sides of Reverus' head and started saying something under his breath. Azailia couldn't hear what he was saying. Small amounts of energy began surging through Reverus' temples, and he started to convulse. His back arched up as the energy went through his body. The soldiers forced him back down. The energy stopped, and Reverus' body went limp. Azailia's face became white. She put her hand over her mouth to prevent any noise from escaping.

The Pravicus said something to the soldiers. When he stopped speaking, they immediately made their way to the door. They exited and walked toward the center of town. The Pravicus remained next to Reverus. He grabbed a wet towel and placed it on Reverus' forehead. The Pravicus smacked Reverus across the face, waking him up. He slowly sat up with the help of the Pravicus.

"What happened?" Reverus stuttered, his eyes rolling back into his head.

"We cured you. You had a grave illness, and we got rid of it."

"Oh," Reverus said, uncertain. "Well, thank you."

The Pravicus smiled and helped him stand up. Azailia was shocked. It didn't seem like a cure. It seemed like torture to her. She watched as they both got up and made their way to the door. Reverus thanked the Pravicus again, and they both left to the center of town.

Azailia followed at a distance, taking a different route to the center so she wouldn't be seen. She arrived just before them. Azailia looked around and saw that almost the whole town had shown up and was crowding the stage. Reverus and the Pravicus went up onto the stage. Azailia faded in the back, hoping to not be noticed.

Reverus walked to the center of the stage, Azailia noticed a guard was on each side of him. "I have wonderful news," he paused, looking at the Pravicus, who nodded. "The Pravicus has cured me of a grave disease." His voice was monotone. "The Pravicus has graciously offered to see everyone for free on their first visit. Over the next week or two, you will all be able to get checkups." Reverus turned and walked to the front of the new office and opened the door. "Shall we?" A cheer broke out over the crowd as the Pravicus entered.

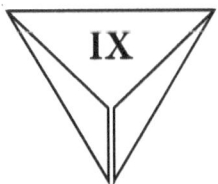

IX

For the rest of the day, the townspeople mulled around excitedly. The guards stood on the outside of the door. One of them had a piece of parchment that he wrote people's names on, setting the time they would be seen. One by one, they would walk up to the guard, he would write something down and then motion for the next.

Irritated, Azailia returned to her home. She couldn't stand it anymore. People were just flocking to see the Pravicus, even if they didn't have issues. The day went by very quickly. When nightfall came, there was a knock at her door. She grabbed a knife from the table and held it so it was concealed behind her arm. She opened the door slightly and there stood Rose. Azailia sighed and let her in.

"I thought you would be at the Pravicus' office like everyone else," Azailia said, defeated.

"Nah, I am going tomorrow. They couldn't fit me in today. Besides, I was hoping you would come with me." Rose's eyes pleading.

Azailia laughed, "Why would I go? Nothing's wrong with me."

"Yeah me neither, but I'm going to get checked anyway."

"That doesn't even make sense, Rose. Why would you need to go to a doctor if you know nothing's wrong?" Azailia shot, her temper rising.

Rose looked down, "But what if something's wrong and I don't know it?"

Azailia threw her hands up in the air, frustrated. "Listen," she calmed her voice. She grabbed Rose by the arms and sat down with her. "I need to tell you something. Something is weird about this guy." Rose looked up, her interest rising. "This afternoon, I went to talk to Reverus. I found him in his office with the Pravicus. Guards were holding him down and the Pravicus was sending small amounts of energy into his head."

"Yeah, he did say the Pravicus cured him of a disease," Rose interjected.

"I know, Rose, but listen. Something's not right here. Just promise me you won't go tomorrow. Come back in the morning, and we'll figure things out, okay?" Azailia insisted, her eyes boring into Rose's. Rose nodded. "Promise me. Say it."

"I promise," Rose finally said. She left shortly after. Azailia felt much better after that. She was glad she had someone she could talk to about this. She wished her parents were back. They would know what to do.

The next morning, there was a knock at the door. She ran to it, expecting Rose. Two black shadows pushed their way through the door and grabbed her by each of her arms. She was pulled farther into her house. They threw her on the ground and started to kick her. She tried to shield her face, but it didn't help. Finally, she just curled into a fetal position. They grabbed her and stood her up. She hung on their arms, unable to stand, blood running down her face. The door opened again and in walked the Pravicus, smiling his twisted smile.

"Azailia, I'm sorry. This is the only way. You need help. You are suffering from *Nome*." She felt a shiver through her body. His voice was disgustingly sweet. Azailia tried to struggle, but her body had lost all feeling. "Bring her," the Pravicus said and turned and walked out. The two carried her, practically dragging her back into the center of the town.

People in town looked at her with worried faces. The Pravicus just nodded to them and assured them that she was sick. She tried to talk, to scream, but her mouth wouldn't move. In fact, she couldn't move any of her body. It was as if it were frozen.

They walked into the center of town and went inside the Pravicus' office. They laid her on the table, and the guards exited the room. Azailia still had no feeling in her body. No matter how hard she tried, she couldn't move. The Pravicus moved behind her.

"Don't worry, this won't last too long." He placed his hands on each side of her temples. There was a huge gust of wind, and Azailia heard the word "Relaisser" in her mind. The Pravicus didn't seem to notice, but Azailia realized she could move again. Using all the force she could muster, she spun around and kicked the Pravicus across the head, throwing him into the wall. He went limp.

Azailia knew the guards would come in any second, so she ran to the side of the door. Before she could exit, the guards entered. Upon seeing the Pravicus on the floor, they drew their swords and advanced towards her. When one of the guards got close enough, she spun around, kicking him back into his partner. His partner sidestepped and charged her, sword raised. She ducked under his arm and flipped him over. Another guard charged inside, sword drawn. Azailia dodged left. The other two guards had stood back up, and all three of them stood blocking the exits but didn't move.

Azailia didn't know what they were waiting for, but she enjoyed the quick rest. It allowed her to gain some strength back. She heard a stir beside her and turned. There stood the Pravicus. He had changed dramatically. His eyes had turned black, and energy was spinning around him. His hands were in front of him, dark energy bouncing back and forth between them. Azailia stood transfixed.

Without any warning, the Pravicus launched the dark energy at her. Azailia closed her eyes, threw her hands in front of her and cried out, "Protectus!" The energy crashed into an invisible shield, causing the room to shake. When she opened her eyes again, she noticed the energy was being deflected. A clear shield was dispersing the energy away from her.

The Pravicus released a surprised laugh. "An elf. How interesting." A wide smile appeared on his face.

"And you're not a doctor."

"How perceptive," his voice hissed. Azailia dropped to her knees as the attack continued from the Pravicus. Her body was weakening and she was losing strength. She started to panic as her shield started weakening. She had to think of something soon.

Her arms gave out, her head was light, and her shield disappeared. The Pravicus stopped his attack and walked over to her. "So sorry it had to end this way, you disgusting elf." He raised his arm as a light appeared in his palm. Azailia braced herself as her eyes started to blur. Before she lost all vision, there was a blinding light, and she heard a scream. Then, everything went dark.

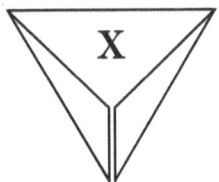

X

Azailia jerked as she felt her body bouncing up and down. She was not sure what was going on, but she did not open her eyes just yet. For a little while, she just listened, continuing to pretend to be unconscious. She heard two voices—a man's followed by a woman's. She could not make out what they were saying. They seemed to be talking about her. Azailia's body tensed as she tried to focus her senses, but her head was pounding and she was weak.

She concentrated a little harder, doing what her father had taught her.

"She's okay. We got there just in time," the man said.

"Are you sure?" said the woman, full of concern. "She looks so pale." The voices sounded so familiar. Finally, her mind clicked.

She opened her eyes and cried out, "Mother! Father!" The sunlight overwhelmed her eyes, and she quickly shut them again. The bouncing had stopped. She opened her eyes a little slower, allowing them time to adjust. That's when she realized she was riding a horse. Her parents had stopped their horses.

"Azailia," Delia said pleasantly. Azailia looked at her parents. They both looked worn, as if they hadn't slept in some time. Her attention went to blood on her father's arm.

"Don't worry, it's not as bad as it looks," he said calmly, noticing her concern.

"What happened? Where are we...?" Azailia asked anxiously, remembering what had happened earlier.

"In due time," her mother answered. "First, are you okay to keep moving?" Azailia nodded. "Good, then we'll explain while we ride." Azailia nodded again, and the three of them set off.

As soon as they were moving at a good pace, her father turned to her. "When we left that night, we rode out towards the blinding light we all saw. We realized that the light had occurred near the road to Gusta. When we arrived, we found a horrendous sight. Hundreds of dead bodies were strewn everywhere. We examined them closer and realized it was a mix of Drutas and the king's men. It seemed a big battle had raged, and it was ended by magicians as quickly as it started, which was the light we had seen. We traveled quickly to Gusta and heard rumor that wars had started to break out all over the land. Towns had begun fighting each other." He paused, taking a breath.

"We decided we needed to find out more. We asked around the town, checking the local taverns and talking to as many people as we could without drawing attention. We didn't make much progress; the people seemed ... out of it." Harrus paused again, his eyes wandering as he thought.

"There had to be something—a cause or a reason all of this had started. It was very difficult, but we finally found one common thing. The king had dispatched envoys for each town and city. With them came the

Pravicus." His eyes went dark, as if he was experiencing the moment again, then continued, "So, that's where we started. We went to check out the advisor. He seemed to be okay, so we turned our attention to the Pravicus. We watched him for a while. He mostly just talked to people, but some of his other methods were more extreme," he looked at Azailia directly, "as you have seen first hand." She gulped, remembering what she had witnessed.

"We received word that one had reached our town, and we departed immediately. When returned to Itaear, we didn't find you at the house. We searched around and finally found you. You were at the Pravicus' place, and we were able to interfere just in time. He fought us off, but we managed to get out of there, with you alive. Unfortunately, the Pravicus is still alive and in the town—"

"What!" Azailia interrupted when she heard this. "We can't just leave him there. What about all the people? We have to help."

"I'm sorry. We can't do anything right now, he's too powerful even for us," her father said. "We'll return though. Don't worry."

Azailia and her parents continued to ride and recount both experiences. Harrus and Delia seemed very proud when Azailia told them about the shield she had put up. Harrus had taught Azailia how to use the shield in one of their training sessions. It was simple magic, but it was definitely useful.

By dusk, they had entered the Mintual Forest. It was almost pitch black when they made camp. They set up just inside the forest so they had cover from any curious eyes.

Azailia's body was exhausted and sore as they finally

settled in. Every time she trained with her father and used the shield, she had been very exhausted. This time, she had used it much longer and to resist other magic. She passed out as soon as she lay down, feeling safe for the first time in a few days.

She awoke the next morning from the warmth of sunlight on her face. Her parents were already up, assuming they had even gone to sleep. Her father had made a fire and was cooking meat.

"Smells good. I'm starving," she said with a yawn as she stretched.

"Just about done." He pulled it off the fire and handed her a piece. She ate it fast, not giving it time to cool. Her father just stared at her in awe as he blew on his to cool it off. "Hungry were you?" he said as he offered her more.

She smiled, a little embarrassed, took some more and ate it more slowly. Her mother joined them minutes later and ate her fill. When they were all fed, they mounted their horses and continued deeper into the forest.

This forest, Azailia noticed, was no ordinary forest. Everything seemed alive. The trees seemed to speak to each other as they swayed back and forth in the wind, not to mention how they towered above them. They practically touched the clouds. The whole forest was alive with motion. Not one thing seemed to be still. In addition, the forest was greener than anything she had ever seen. In fact, as she looked around, there was not one brown leaf.

As they went deeper into the forest, it became darker, not because the sun was going down but because the trees became thicker and thicker, blocking out the sky. Shadows started to appear dancing on the ground as the trees swayed back and forth. Out of the corner of Azailia's eyes, she saw something jump from one tree to another.

She turned her head to focus on the area, but it was still.

"Did you guys see that?" she said as her heart started racing.

Her mom turned. "See what, sweetie?"

It must have been a shadow, she thought. A few moments later, she saw it again. This time she was sure of it.

"There it is again," she said, pointing. Her parents looked and then shook their heads. She became very alert. Something was out there, and she knew it. The wind around them picked up, leaves showering down on them. The horses stopped and began stomping their feet. Something was aggravating them. Azailia reached for her sword by habit but grabbed nothing. She felt naked without a weapon. She looked around her, and everything seemed to be moving towards her. Her parents remained motionless in front of her. But they seemed very alert, and their hands were on the hilts of their swords.

They sat still for what seemed like forever. The only noise was the wind blowing and the horses pawing at the ground. An odd plant grabbed Azailia's attention. This plant had two roots. It shot up the side of a tree and then split in two parts, which then wrapped around the tree. She followed the vine until she found the top. Here, smaller vines seemed to cascade down the trunk. She focused harder. She could not make out what was odd about this plant. Then she saw it—two eyes stared directly back at her from the top of the plant. The parts that wrapped around the tree began to unwrap, and the whole plant disconnected from the tree.

She gasped as she realized it wasn't a plant. It was a person. Fear entered into her immediately. She looked around and realized all the plants were coming alive.

Seconds later, Azailia and her parents were surrounded by at least twenty people. All of them looked different. They were all painted with different colors. Some had branches on their arms that were fixed to the front of their hands, completely covering them. One even had leaves all over his body, camouflaging him completely. Azailia, although scared, could not help but admire this ability.

She could not tell if they were real people or part of nature. She had heard stories of a mystical forest where the trees came alive when threatened, but she thought it was just a story.

As she studied the things more closely, she was able to make out fingers. She realized that these were just people. This did not help her fear at all though. She looked at her parents as they were getting off their horses. Azailia was still frozen; she did not know what to do. She knew in combat situations she had a better chance of surviving if she was on a horse and the enemy was on foot. It was about elevation.

One of the biggest of the plant people walked up to her parents. When the man was directly in front of her father, he stopped.

"Freo Infinitas Fur," Harrus said softly. Azailia recognized the old language. It was rarely used these days except for magic. The man nodded.

With incredible speed, the man drew a dagger and threw it in their direction. Instinctively, Azailia raised her arms over her face. A tear escaped from her eyes as she heard a man groan then a body hit the ground. Her fear was replaced by anger as she burned with rage. She opened her eyes, crouching down, readying herself for a fight.

To her surprise, her father stood unharmed. Azailia spun around and saw a man in black lying on the ground, blood running from under his body. Her anger dissipated as fast as it had come, and she wiped the tears away.

"Do not fear, young one," said a voice. It seemed to surround her. Azailia realized it was coming from the man in front of her father. "This man has been following you for some time now. We have been tracking him. Your father also knew, but I told him not to do anything. Now, before we talk more, let's go somewhere less open. It is still unsafe here." He turned to the other men surrounding them and shouted, "Retorner."

As one, the others faded back into the forest, disappearing just as they had appeared. Azailia was amazed. Even though she looked right where one had disappeared, she couldn't make out the person.

"Let's move," he said quietly. He turned and started to go but then paused. He looked up at the sky peering through the trees. He then looked at the horses and raised his hand. "Lucere." A single light erupted from his hand and rested in front of the three horses.

"That's better," he said, then turned and led the way.

Her mother looked at Azailia and smiled with a wink. "Don't worry. You'll know what's happening soon." They knew she was confused but did not say any more.

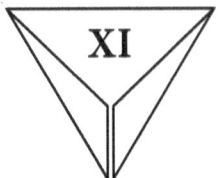

XI

They moved quickly through the forest, at least as fast as the horses could move through the condensing trees. The man leading them seemed to float through the forest; his feet barely touched the ground, and he created no sound as he moved swiftly. The only sound was the crunching made by the three horses.

It must have been very late at night when they finally stopped moving. The trees had become slightly more sparse. The moon shined brightly through the trees, creating pools of light on the forest floor. The man had stopped for a minute and squatted down to the ground. He looked around and then stood up again.

"We're almost there. Let's keep moving." And he continued on his path, but at a slower pace. They continued to travel in silence. Azailia gazed at the night sky through the blanket of treetops. There were thousands of stars trying to break through the trees and gaze upon the forest floor. It seemed to be a game the trees and stars played. Occasionally, one would break through for a moment, but the trees would catch it and block it out again.

Azailia found this entertaining, letting herself be distracted. They traveled for a few more hours. The trees became less and less dense until, up ahead of the group, the trees stopped. The sun was just coming up, and it illuminated a huge mass behind the trees. An enormous mountain grew out of the ground and up into the clouds. Azailia looked to the left and right and could not see an end. It was as if the mountain had become the horizon.

They exited the forest a few minutes later. In front of them stood the huge mountain. Azailia's mouth dropped. It was bigger than she had thought. The top of the mountain wasn't even visible as it disappeared into the heavens.

They all stopped at the base of the mountain as the man walked straight up to the foot of it. Azailia watched with curiosity. There was no way to climb the huge mass. The surface was unnaturally smooth. He placed a single hand on it, closed his eyes and muttered, "Upana." A few seconds went by as nothing occurred. The man backed away.

A few more seconds passed, and when the whole mountain started to shake, which in turn, caused the ground beneath them to tremble. The area where the man had touched illuminated bright green. From the handprint, cracks of green light weaved out in every direction. The cracks curled up, down and sideways. Once they reached a certain point, they shot out in both directions, perpendicular to the original line. They curved down and around until they all connected.

Azailia looked at the shape and realized it was a door. The cracks started to bleed, filling the entire shape in the green light. Once the entire shape was full, the green light faded, revealing a tunnel. It led directly through the mountain. On the other side, Azailia saw buildings and people moving about. There was an entire city protected by these mountains.

Her face must have shown her surprise because her

mother spoke up. "That is exactly how I reacted the first time I saw this. It's amazing, isn't it?" Azailia didn't make any reply. She just stared in amazement. The man and her parents urged their horses forward through the tunnel, and Azailia slowly followed, in awe of what she was seeing. As soon as she passed through, the part behind her immediately became solid again. She hurried her horse once she saw this.

When all four of them were through to the other side, the entire tunnel disappeared. In its place, the mountain had regrown. The only evidence was an outline of the tunnel. She looked up and down the mountain range, noticing it circled the entire place.

"Welcome," the man said, regaining Azailia's attention, "to Sarvah. My name is Weisen." He bowed as he said this. "This is the largest hidden city. We remain separate from the Capitol, and as I have heard, you now know why." His eyes settled on Azailia. "We survive outside of the king's thumb because of things we have learned. If you follow me, I'll explain more."

As they walked, Azailia stared at everything. The place was huge. Towards the center of town, there were tall buildings and houses. North of them were hills with farmlands cast over them, while to the south there was a beautiful building with flowers exploding all over its sides. All the buildings seemed to be built from the ground. In fact, the buildings actually grew out of the ground. Thousands of roots shot out of the ground to form walls and then grew even higher to form roofs, sometimes even a second floor. The roofs were covered with leaves that grew from the limbs. It was definitely an odd sight.

Another thing that caught Azailia's eyes were the people. The majority were dressed extremely well. Their clothes fit neatly to their bodies, and no one wore clothes too big for them. Azailia felt a little embarrassed because her clothes were ragged from so much travel. No one seemed to notice though. As she looked closer, she noticed something that made her heart leap. The people walking around were ... Elves—at least most of them were! She had wondered many times if her family was the last of their kind. She had heard rumors but knew nothing for sure.

"This way," Weisen said and turned south toward the larger building.

"What is that place?" she said in awe as she pointed at the building they were headed to. "It's beautiful!"

Weisen turned and smiled. "Yes it is. That's where all the high officials live and work. We call it the Torr, which means, 'The Watchtower'." Azailia just stared in awe. Everything was so surreal, and the fact that Elves were now a reality made her overjoyed.

When they got to the Torr's main entrance, two guards blocked their path. Weisen said a few words Azailia could not understand, but it made the guards allow them passage. The inside of the Torr was much different than the outside. The walls were just like any normal walls, not the earthy look the outside had.

It was extremely beautiful. Near the top, where the walls and ceiling met, were great arches that connected the two. This first area was very long. There was a table about half the length of the room in the middle. Many decorative chairs surrounded it. All of them were empty.

Weisen turned to them. "I'm sorry, young lady, if I startled you earlier." This was directed at Azailia. "I'm the leader's right hand. I didn't make time for formal intro-ductions earlier as I had strict instructions to return with you safely and with haste. We're meeting a man named

Outen. He'll get you all situated. In fact, here he comes now." Weisen looked down one of the halls that jutted off to the left of the main hall, and walking down it was a stocky man. He had a beard and curly hair, wore simple leather clothing, and he carried no weapon.

"Harrus!" Outen said in a gruff voice. Harrus smiled back, and they met in a strong embrace. "How are you doing? It's been a while, my old friend."

"I'm good. It's good to see you again too! You remember my wife, Delia?" Harrus replied heartily.

"Of course, how could I forget such a beautiful woman?" Outen bowed and kissed Delia's hand. She greeted him with a smile. "And you must be the beautiful Azailia," he said, spotting her.

Azailia shyly replied, "Yes sir. It's nice to meet you." She extended her hand. Outen laughed and pulled Azailia into a hug. She awkwardly hugged back.

"Anyway," Outen continued, releasing Azailia, "I'm sure you're all hungry by now." Azailia, at that point, realized how hungry she actually was and nodded enthusiastically. "I knew you would be. Follow me." Before leaving, Harrus nodded to Weisen.

"Thank you for everything, Weisen," Harrus said. Weisen bowed his head in acknowledgement.

"Come on, y'all." Outen gestured for them to follow and led them down the hall where he had come from. This hall, just like the main one, looked completely normal and unlike the outside. They didn't walk long before they turned and entered a big room. In this room, a long table stood in the middle with many chairs around it. On the table was an enormous amount of food. There was steak, pork and chicken. Other plates had beans, corn and cabbage and many other foods, including sweets.

Before Azailia even moved towards the table, her mouth started watering. They made their way over to the table and sat down. Outen sat at the end with Azailia on one side and her parents on the other. While they loaded their plates and ate, there was no talking, just the constant noise of chewing. People also kept coming in and filling up their mugs with whatever drink they wanted.

When they all slowed down, Outen finally spoke. "So, this is what's going to happen. Salvator is expecting to speak with you," he said, addressing Harrus and Delia. "He'll want to speak to you after we get Azailia situated."

"What do you mean? Who's Salvator?" Azailia questioned.

"Don't worry, we'll tell you everything tomorrow. For now, finish eating, and I'll show you where you can get some sleep. You'll need your rest for what's to come. I'll come get you in the morning. But for now, let's just chat. How was your trip here?" And from then until they finished eating, they simply talked and reminisced about old stories.

Azailia didn't realize how long Outen and her parents had known each other—apparently since they were kids. It was fun to hear the stories from back in the day.

They finally finished eating and decided it would be best to rest up. Outen led the three out of the dining room and down the hall a little farther. They turned down another hallway, which had many more doors than the last. Outen took them to the one at the far end. This was the most secluded. It didn't have another door next to it like the others. Outen opened the door and led them in. This room had three sections. It had a main bed for Harrus and Delia and another bed in a separate room for Azailia. In the center was a small sitting area, and connected to that was a room to wash up.

"I think you'll find fitted clothes in the closets, and anything else you need, just find me. For now, get some sleep, and I'll see you in the morning." Harrus, Delia and Azailia all said goodnight, and Outen left.

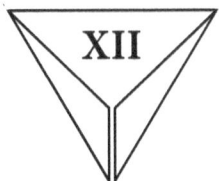

XII

"So…," Azailia said as soon as Outen left, her face dedicated, "are you two going to explain now?"

"Well," her father answered, choosing his words carefully before he spoke, "things are starting to change. We don't know much, but I believe we'll learn a lot tomorrow." He paused. "Do you have any specific questions?"

Azailia thought for a moment, feeling as though she were being brushed off. She could tell her father knew more than he was letting on. She looked at her mother, whose eyes were cast down to the floor. "Actually, yes." One question burned in her mind. "I thought we were the last of our race, but … out there…" She pointed at the door. "Why didn't I know this?"

Her family had always been secretive of their heritage. Elves had all but disappeared when the dragons left. They had always been very careful about hiding who they truly were. As a result, she always felt alone. Constantly using magic to conceal her ears and always trying to blend in had been her life. Her closest friend was Rose, and she didn't even know the truth. To find out about this was a relief, but it also angered her. A small amount of anger overflowed into her voice. "Every time I asked you about our race, you never told me about this. And yet you knew all along! Why?"

"Sweetie," Delia said as she stood up and placed a hand on Azalia's shoulder, which she immediately shrugged off, "it was for your own protection. We needed to keep you safe," her mother said, concern filling her voice. Azailia didn't look at her. She felt betrayed by them. They had been lying to her the whole time.

She regained a little composure and looked at her parents. "Okay," she said as a lead to another question, "what is this place?"

Her mother and father looked at each other. "Sit down," her father said softly, patting the open spot beside him. As she sat, he continued, "We are—"

"Are you sure, Harrus?" her mother interrupted.

He smiled, "It's time she knows the truth. Azailia," he turned to look at her, his face serious, "this is the main camp of the Drutas."

Azailia shot up. "Wha…" she stuttered, "what do you mean the Drutas?" her words coming out with a mix of anger, fear and nervousness, her eyes darting to the door.

"Azailia, calm down," her father said in a soothing tone. "It's not what you think. All the information you know is wrong. Let me explain. Sit down." Azailia slowly retook her seat. "To start off, do you remember the story about the Thirteen Chosen?" Azailia nodded. "Okay, good. So the Thirteen left to train with the Dragons. When they returned, they took over as advisors to the king.

"One day, an announcement was made—the Thirteenth Chosen had killed the other twelve and fled. A bounty was placed on the Thirteenth. A couple months later, a group known as the Drutas had surfaced. They were immediately labeled as rebels. A rumor quickly spread—the Thirteenth was the leader of this new group."

Again, Azailia nodded, unsure where he was going with this. "Well, this was incorrect. After some investigation, we found out that the king had the twelve murdered, and the Thirteenth had escaped and been framed for the murder. The one true part is that, yes, he does lead the Drutas, which, in case you didn't know, means True."

Azailia shook her head in disbelief.

Her parents had never told her anything about this. In fact, they were pretty secretive about their own past. This would explain why. But how could everything she had learned growing up been false? She thought back to all the times she had heard about the Drutas—all the evil they were doing, all the towns they were attacking.

"It can't be true," she said shakily. "I don't believe you. All of the things they have don—"

"No," her father said, pounding his fist down. "Think about it. When have you actually seen proof of them doing harm?" He paused, and she shook her head, but it did get her thinking. "Now think about all the times harm has come from the kingdom. You just experienced it. Come on, you know exactly what I'm talking about."

"...the Pravicus," she said quietly and slumped in her chair. It all clicked. When she looked at the facts of what she knew, rather than what she was told, it made sense. The Drutas weren't the enemies. The kingdom was ... the Pravicus was!

"How could they?" she asked rhetorically. Her reality had been shattered. In one night, her entire world had changed. All emotions had left her. She just sat there, numb. It was too much to process. Her parents sat with her a little longer in silence.

"Listen," her mother finally broke the silence, "I know this is a lot to process. Let's turn in for the night.

Tomorrow, we'll answer your questions, and all will become clear." Azailia nodded reluctantly and slowly retreated to her room.

Azailia's mind was racing. She couldn't believe how blind she had been. All she needed to do was open her eyes and look at the damage and who was *actually* causing it, not what the appearance was.

"Time to wake up," she heard her mother's voice say. Azailia opened her eyes groggily and saw her mother standing above her. She grunted and rubbed her eyes. She didn't even remember falling asleep. She sat up in bed and rubbed the remaining sleep out of her eyes as her mother left. When she was a little more awake, she walked to the closet and opened it.

Her eyes widened. Hanging in the closet were some of the most beautiful clothes she had ever seen. There were several tunics of different colors. One was pink with a white trim. Another was dark brown with a gold trim. They all had embroidery running up and down. There were also several matching leather leggings. Another outfit looked like it was made for training. It had thick leather trousers with a sleeveless leather vest. There were also many others, including dozens of shoes and boots.

She grabbed a light brown tunic and matching leggings. A pair of black boots caught her eye. She grabbed them and made her way to the washroom. Her parents were still in their room as she came downstairs. She closed the door of the washroom and stripped her clothes. The bath was full of fresh warm water. As she slipped into the bath, the warmth spread through her entire body. She used a cloth to cleanse herself. As the grime washed away, her flawless skin reappeared.

Feeling refreshed, she grabbed a towel and pulled

herself out of the bath. She dried herself off, tied her hair back and dressed. When she was finished, she turned to leave but caught herself in the mirror. She barely recognized herself. Here stood a very beautiful woman. Her features had sharpened and her hair was longer. She was stunning.

She walked out of the washroom, and her parents were both standing there. Her father was wearing a fairly plain outfit—a pair of black pants and white shirt with a coat on top. The coat was form-fitted and ended just above his ankles. Her mother was wearing a white dress with a sash tied around her waist. She looked amazing.

"Good morning," Azailia greeted them.

"Good morning to you too," her mother said, hugging her. "How are you feeling?"

"Much better. A much needed sleep and bath," she replied cheerily. There was a knock at the door. Harrus opened it.

"Greetings Outen," he said as Outen walked in.

"Greetings," he said with a bow. "Was everything satisfactory?"

"Oh yes, everything was great." Azailia answered, surprising herself at the ease with which she spoke.

"Excellent. Then let's eat; you must be hungry," Outen replied cheerfully and led them back down the hall to the main room. The atmosphere had changed. The hall was a lot busier now. People roamed all over; some scurried across the hall into other rooms while others walked slowly, reading books. People nodded to them as they passed.

Outen curved back into the room they had eaten in the previous night. It had the exact setup as the night before, except this time the tables were filled with mounds of fresh fruit, sausages, and bread and butter. Fresh juice was in a pitcher on the table. They took their seats and began eating.

When they were finished, Outen led them to a completely new room. People were already there. One was reading some maps, and another was sitting at a table studying a book. When the man reading the maps saw Outen, he stood up and smiled. "It's about time," he said jovially.

"Oh, calm down," Outen replied with a wave. "They had to eat. We're here now." Outen smiled and turned to Azailia. "This is Zeigen. Now, have a seat."

Zeigen was a good-looking guy. He was lean but muscular. He had short dark hair and a clean face. He had hazel eyes. Though soft, they held tons of experience.

"So, this is the famous Azailia," Zeigen said as he looked her. "I've heard a lot about you, young lady."

"Zeigen," Outen said to Azailia, "is one of our best trainers. Magic, sword, bow—you name it. He's legendary."

"Nice to meet you," Azailia said as she nodded.

"Well, we have a lot to do today, so, Harrus, Delia," Outen directed his attention to them, "you two will be meeting with Salvator a little later. Azailia," he turned to her again, "if it's all right with you, Zeigen has graciously offered to train you. How does that sound?"

She thought about it momentarily; everything was happening so fast, she just needed something stable to grab onto. The training could be that. If she were trained, regardless of what occurred, she would be more prepared.

"I accept. But can I ask one thing?" She thought now was as good as any. Outen nodded. "What's really happening out there?" Her implication was clear.

Outen sighed, "Well, I guess at this point you might as well know everything. I'm sure your parents cleared some things up last night?" Azailia nodded. "Okay, that makes things a little easier. Here's what has been happening. The king has sent the Pravicus to each town in order to control people. They are using a technique where they send small amounts of energy through one's brain. They've been teaching people that, with this, they can remove certain tendencies and evil purposes from their soul. In actuality, it destroys part of the brain and, in turn, lowers their ability to operate fully."

Azailia was appalled, her mouth hanging open in shock.

"So all those soldiers, the ones with the blank faces?" she managed to say.

"Exactly. They've been altered to be more 'manageable' as they put it."

Nausea began to overcome Azailia, and she felt like she might vomit. She grabbed a cup of water and sipped it, fighting back the sensation growing in her stomach. The fact that someone would do such brutal things to another appalled her.

"So," Outen continued, "we want you to train with Zeigen and help us win this war. What do you think?"

She slammed her empty cup down, her mind made. "Let's do this!"

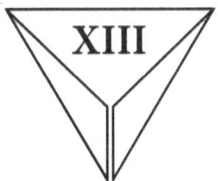

XIII

Azailia stood facing Zeigen, both holding their swords. The hill they stood on was just on the outskirts of the city. Behind them was a small grouping of trees, and through that, Azailia thought she could make out water. Zeigen had led her up here to start her training. The sun was high in the sky with not a cloud to be seen. In the distance, Azailia could see the ripple of heat sitting on the ground. She squinted her eyes and waited. Zeigen looked relaxed and unfazed by the bright sun. A slight breeze picked up, blowing her hair as Zeigen lunged at her. She brought her sword up, deflected his advance and lunged back with a quick attack. Zeigen easily blocked and countered. Spinning quickly, he smacked her on the calf with the flat of his sword. She stumbled slightly but was able to recover.

He's so fast, she thought for a moment. Then, with a twist of her body, she lunged at him. Right before she was blocked, she slid to the right and jabbed at his side. Seconds before the sword made contact, Zeigen moved with amazing speed and ended up behind her with his sword on the back of her neck. She stood frozen, shocked that he moved that fast. She knew Elven warriors were fast, but she had no idea they were this fast. She turned around to see that Zeigen was just smiling.

"Good!" he said, no disappointment in his voice. "Your biggest problem is you focus too much on what's in front of you rather than using your surroundings to your advantage." Azailia tried to smile, but she did not feel that she did "good". "Next, we'll test your bow skills. I'll return shortly." He took the swords and walked off.

Azailia sat down on the grass and closed her eyes. It was a hot day, even more so now that she just sparred. Beads of sweat slid down her face. The wind picked up, and she turned her face into it, grateful for the cool breeze.

She opened her eyes and looked around. The place was beautiful. The Torr sat behind her, the flowers glowing in the sun. She could practically smell the fragrance they gave off. In front of her was a large forest spreading back to what she thought was water. Near the Torr, the town was bustling, people running all around.

Zeigen returned a few minutes later carrying a bow and a full quiver of arrows. "Follow me," he said as he walked by her. She followed him towards the trees. When she got close, she saw that dummies had been set up on the tree line. Zeigen stopped and handed her the bow. "Ok, this should be easy. Shoot the dummies."

Azailia looked at the bow. It was beautiful. It looked hand carved. It curved back on both ends and then curved in reverse just before the string. It had carvings around the entire handle from the lower limb all the way up to the upper limb. She held it up and was shocked at how light it was.

"I think I can do that." She confidently nocked an arrow, aimed and fired. The bow was not like the ones she was used to. This was much lighter and way more powerful. The arrow sailed.

"Shit," she cursed. Zeigen looked at her surprised.

"What?" she snapped, her frustration building. "I'm used to a heavier bow." She grabbed another arrow, took a minute to aim, breathed out slowly, and loosed the arrow. It hit the dummy straight through the head. She lowered the bow and smiled confidently.

"Very well done!" Zeigen praised. "Now, a moving target." He waved his hand, and a dummy started moving back and forth between two trees. Again, she nocked an arrow, led the target and loosed the arrow. It flew through the air and lodged itself in the dummy's arm.

"Not bad at all. You'll be a skilled archer in no time." He waved his hand again, and the dummy stopped moving. "Now, let's see what you can do with magic. Zeigen led her back up the hill. "I want you to do some basic maneuvers if you can. First, I want you to create fire in your hand."

Azailia agreed and raised her hand, palm up. She concentrated, drawing energy into her hand. "Ignis," she said. A small flame appeared in her hand for a few seconds and then disappeared.

"Excellent!" Zeigen said happily. "Now, can you create water?"

Azailia nodded, concentrating the energy again. "Hydor." A ball of water appeared in her hand, although it wasn't very controlled. It continued to alter shapes and drip from the sides of her hand until it had all fallen to the ground and vanished.

"Amazing!" Zeigen said. "You're way more experienced in magic than I had expected. Okay, now for a slightly harder one. I want you to raise a part of the earth up."

Azailia was exhausted. Her energy was draining quickly. She had never raised earth before. She didn't think it would be too hard. She placed her hand, palm down this time. "Erda." The ground started to shake beneath her hand. Pieces of it began to rise as she concentrated harder. Sweat appeared on her forehead the more she concentrated. Her body began to give out. She fell to one knee, releasing the energy, her body exhausted.

"Amazing!" he exclaimed. "Now do you know why you feel the way you do?" Her body felt so heavy, it took everything she had just to shake her head. "The energy you use to cast the spell comes directly from you, or your spirit so to speak. It's a part of you that you create into another form. Just like a muscle, it can become stronger with practice. However, if you use too much of it at one time, it can exhaust or even kill you. It's not to be taken lightly. Most of the time, your body will lose consciousness before this can occur. There have been times when a spell continued after the person had lost consciousness, but that is rare. You can also learn to draw energy from other living things." Zeigen looked around, the sun had started to set. "I think that's enough for the day. Why don't you go get something to eat and rest. We'll meet here in the morning."

Azailia did not realize how late it had gotten. She took a moment to catch her breath. She bowed to Zeigen and made her way back.

Sitting at the table already were her parents and Outen. They smiled when they saw her.

"How was your day? You look exhausted," her father said, noticing her sluggish movements.

Azailia settled into the free chair beside her mother and pulled a plate over to her. "It was, and I am," she said, her face drained. "All he did was test me today. He is fast! I didn't even get close to hitting him." They laughed. Even though she was exhausted, she couldn't help but join in. It felt good to laugh again. Things had finally seemed to loosen, and she relaxed.

When Azailia and her parents were back in their room, her father turned to her, "So, we need to tell you something." She looked at him. "We are leaving tomorrow for a little while."

"What … already? We just got here," Azailia complained.

"Unfortunately, it's necessary. We received an urgent message, and we have to go meet with a contact. Don't worry, we won't be away long."

"We'll be gone before you get up, so don't worry. Besides, you probably won't even notice. You'll be too busy training." Azailia smiled even though her eyes showed sadness, and she hugged her parents. She lingered a little with her mom before they went off to bed.

Azailia rose the next morning to find her parents had already left. She dressed in her training gear and made her way towards the mess hall. As she walked through the main hall, a reflection caught her eye. She turned and realized the sun was bouncing off one of the chairs. She shielded her eyes and saw that there was a metallic symbol engraved in the top of the chair.

She walked over and traced her fingers over the symbol. It was in the shape of a dragon. The dragon was facing left and his tail curled behind him, almost forming a circle. His wing expanded behind him. In the circle were two circles connected in the middle. She didn't recognize the symbol.

"It's our symbol," a voice said. Startled, she jumped back and turned. A very tall man stood in front of her. He had piercing blue eyes, short blonde hair and features any woman would swoon over. Azailia was frozen in place. He was probably the best-looking man she had ever seen. He walked forward and turned to look at the symbol. She turned, watching his every movement. "The Dragon," he ran his slender finger over the curve, "stands for the Gods, or Supremes. The two circles represent infinity. They never end, always starting again. The symbol itself means, 'The Continuation of all Life and the Supremes.'" He turned and smiled at her.

There was a bang as a door closed behind her. She turned to look, but nothing was there. "Who are y—" she started to say, but when she turned back, the man was gone.

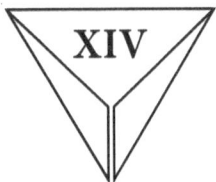

XIV

Azailia met Zeigen at the top of the hill. He was standing there holding two wooden swords. He tossed one to her.

"Before we start, something weird happened this morning," she said to him.

"Hmm...?" he replied, urging her on.

"Well," she didn't want to sound crazy but didn't know how else to say it, "I was in the main hall looking at the symbol that represents the Drutas. I didn't know what it was, when a man appeared out of nowhere and explained it to me. He said the symbol meant," she paused, wanting to duplicate his exact words, "The Continuation of all Life and the Supremes. Then he just vanished."

Zeigen smiled a knowing smile, "That's interesting. Who was he?"

"I don't know. I was hoping you knew." He shook his head. She was just about to dig further when Zeigen lunged at her. She blocked. Clearly the conversation was over.

She trained for the next few weeks, and each day Zeigen would raise the level of difficulty. She noticed her strength and speed increasing. She was able to keep up with Zeigen, or so she thought. She was definitely getting better. She was soon caught off guard when Zeigen tossed her a real sword. It was much lighter than the training swords they had been using.

She was able to hold her own now. Her body seemed to adapt to things a lot quicker. It was almost as if she had learned to predict her opponent. Part of her mind remained on one thing always though—her parents. They had yet to return, each day her mind creating worse and worse reasons why.

As the weeks passed, the thought of her parents grew. The constant worry even interfered with her training. One day, Zeigen let her go early because she wasn't able to focus, and he could tell.

That night as she slept, she was cast into a world of imagination. *She was walking down a corridor, gown blowing in the wind. The door in front of her was wide open, and she could see the sun shining through. As she came closer to the opening, a cheering met her ears. The closer she got, the louder the cheers became. She emerged to find herself on the balcony of a tower. Below her were hundreds of people who were looking up at her and cheering.*

She looked down at herself, and she was in a beautiful gown. She touched her hair and felt a crown. She was queen. Azailia glistened in the sun, her circlet sparkling as the sun hit the many different gems encrusted into it. She raised her hand, and the crowd went silent.

A disturbance stirred in the back of the crowd. Azailia tried to see what it was but couldn't. The disturbance grew louder, and people turned to look. It kept growing and growing until the entire crowd had turned their attention to it.

Curiosity getting the best of her, she went down the stairs and exited the tower. The crowd parted immediately and made a direct line to the disturbance. She walked quickly to the cause of the problem. Two people lie on the ground, face down. She kneeled down and shook them. No movement. She pushed harder. Still nothing. Frantically, she pushed each one onto their back with all her strength.

Seeing the faces, she shimmied backwards, tears pouring from her eyes as she screamed. Lying dead were her parents. Everything went black around her. It was now just her alone with her parents. A hooded man appeared, standing behind her mother and father. He was laughing. Azailia tried to move, but her body was frozen. His eyes glowed through the blackness. A flash of light shot from the man and through Azailia's body. Pain seared through her.

Azailia sat up in her bed, cold sweat running down her body. Her breathing was heavy. She looked around, but all she saw was the faint light from the candle in the corner. She got up and walked to the washroom. She poured some fresh water into the basin and splashed it over her face. She couldn't shake the feeling that something was wrong. She didn't think her parents were dead, but she thought it was a warning of something.

It was still dark outside when she had dressed and made her way out. The sky was illuminated only by the bright moon and the many stars. The only people out at this time were a few patrolmen. They looked at Azailia oddly but continued their rounds.

As she walked through the city, she looked around trying to shake off the dream. She had been walking for about an hour when the sun finally peaked over the horizon.

The sunlight glistened off the fresh dew, and birds began their morning song. Azailia found a nice spot to sit and relax. She had to get her mind off the dream. She remembered Zeigen had taught her the art of Meddwl. It was a technique used to calm the mind and expand the senses. They had practiced often.

"You're tensing," Zeigen had said when he was first teaching her. "You have to relax every part of your body. Don't focus on anything specific. Instead, listen to the sounds of the trees, the birds in the sky. Feel the wind on your face, the ground underneath you." Azailia took slow breaths as she relaxed her body.

"Good," he had said softly. "Now, push your attention out." She had exhaled as she started to sense the people walking through town. The animals playing in the forest until....

"There!" She had jumped up and ran to the spot. She returned a moment later with a small metal ball. "I found it." She handed it to Zeigen as he smiled.

"Well done!"

As she sat with her eyes closed, she expanded her mind. She could feel birds flying around the mountains. She pushed her mind farther, and she could feel the animals behind the mountains in the Mintual Forest. She could even sense the people in her town of Itaear. She tried to search for her parents but could not sense them anywhere. She focused harder until something grabbed her attention. It was a black spot. It was as if the world just disappeared in this area. It was near the Jetra River. Azailia could sense everything around this one spot but she could not make out this area. She pushed against the black spot with all her might.

Help ... Stunned by the sudden voice, she focused harder on the spot. She closed out everything else around it. The spot began to form, and she recognized it as a body. It was just an outline, but definitely a body, and one that spoke to her.

Can you hear me? She tried to reach out to the shape. She received no answer. The body suddenly moved away from her. Her space started to close, and she found herself staring back at the fields in front of her. Her concentration had faltered. She turned and saw Zeigen standing behind her, his hand on her shoulder.

"Zeigen, I have to tell you what just happened," Azailia said frantically.

"It's okay," he said calmly, "I could sense your intensity."

"What do you mean, you could sense my concentration?" she said, getting distracted.

"I could sense your focus. The more skilled you become with your mind, the more you'll be able to sense things, even other people. I couldn't tell you what you saw, but I could feel your distress. Tell me what happened."

She fumbled for words for a minute, caught up in what he had just said and what had happened. "Well, last night I had a dream where I saw my parents dead. A man in a black robe appeared and killed me also." She paused, trying to shed the feeling that had overcome her. "I couldn't shake off the dream, so I came outside to get some air. Then as the sun came up, I decided to do some Meddwl to calm my mind. As my mind expanded, I found a black spot on the Jetra River." Zeigen looked at her intently now. "I'd never seen that before, so I focused harder and that's when I noticed it was a body. And then...," she paused again and looked Zeigen in the eyes, "it said, 'Help....'"

Zeigen seemed to take a minute to think over her story.

"What do you think I should do?" Azailia asked, breaking the silence.

"Well," he paused then turned to her and asked, "what do you think you should do?"

This took her off guard. She looked up at him, confused.

"Well," Zeigen continued, "I have trained you well. You still have much to learn, but I feel confident you can make this decision alone."

A new level of respect for Zeigen grew in Azailia. She hadn't realized how much he thought of her until now.

"I felt drawn to him … at least I think it was a him." She recalled the feeling she had. "I have to go find him," she said suddenly. Zeigen smiled in response.

"Go ready your things, and I'll meet you back here," Zeigen told her. She agreed.

Azailia returned about an hour later to find Zeigen standing there, a horse now behind him.

"I've taught you everything I can at this point," he said with a smile as she walked up to him. "When you return, you'll continue your training with someone else—a specialist so to speak.

"I want you to be careful while you're out. A lot of things have changed since you arrived. Stay out of trouble, and don't put yourself in any situation that you could avoid. We need you back alive. Coming back dead just wouldn't work for me." A wry smile spread across his face. Azailia laughed.

"I have something for you," he said as he reached behind him. He pulled out a beautiful leather sheath and handed it to her. A hilt stuck out of the top. A single pink gem was encrusted in the pommel. It was beautiful. She gripped the hilt, noticing that it fit her hand perfectly, and pulled the blade out. The blade curved as she took it out of the sheath. The sword was flawlessly balanced and a perfect weight for her.

"It's made from the finest Elven steel, layered over ten times," Zeigen explained as she admired the sword. "On the side of the blade," he pointed to a spot near the hilt, "is the name of the sword."

"Pa'Vate," Azailia said under her breath. As soon as she said it, the sword started to glow mildly.

"It means 'purify'."

Azailia smiled widely as she looked back up at Zeigen, "Thank you so much. It's perfect."

She mounted her horse, her new sword at her side. "I promise I'll return," she said with one last smile and then turned towards the exit.

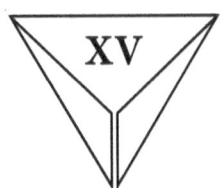

XV

Azailia watched as the tunnel disappeared from the mountain. She was back in the Mintual Forest, alone. She felt different though—calmer, more confident and with a sense of purpose. She pulled the reigns to the right and led the horse away from the mountain entrance.

Her first stop was Itaear; she wanted to return to her town. She didn't have much time, so she sped through the forest. It was much easier this time. Her horse seemed to know exactly how to maneuver through the trees.

As they raced through the forest, she noticed she could sense the movement of the trees in the wind, the movement of animals around her and even the wind as it pushed the leaves over the ground. Her senses had developed even more than she thought. A sense of courage surged through her body. She almost felt invincible. She let her mind wander, fantasizing about being able to take on the strongest of opponents.

Her fantasy was interrupted by Zeigen's voice from before, "Now remember, you're going to have many more abilities when you go out into the world. Don't let that go to your head. There are still people who are stronger than you. One of your biggest strengths is that you're smart." At the time, she had just nodded, understanding his words.

She smiled as she rode, remembering that day. That was the first day she bested Zeigen in a sword fight.

After about five hours of riding, she slowed down and exited the Mintual Forest. She saw smoke on the horizon. She was close now. She slowed her pace as she neared the town. She saw what looked like a wall. As she got closer, she realized that was exactly what it was. A wall had been constructed around the entire town. She brought her horse to a stop, concern filling her body. The wind picked up and blew towards her.

She coughed as the smell of decay filled her nostrils. She used her sleeve to cover her nose and turned away. The smell was unbearable. She led her horse farther north to circle the town. As she turned towards the main road, she heard the gate open. She turned to see a cart coming out. Two soldiers on horseback were dragging the cart out of the town. They turned right, away from her, and kept going until they reached a large pit. The guards jumped off their horses, went to the back of the cart, and together, they heaved several large sacks into the pit. When the cart was empty, they returned to town, and the gate closed.

As soon as the gates were closed, Azailia rode over to the pit, careful not to be seen. As she got closer, the smell got stronger. Birds littered the area. She looked in and immediately had to choke back the urge to vomit. Hundreds of dead bodies had been tossed in the pit—some with dismembered limbs and some with boils or some other growth. Flies covered the bodies while birds picked at the rotting flesh. It was hideous. She turned away, unable to look anymore as the bile began to build in her throat again.

She heard the gates opening again, so she quickly moved to a small patch of trees close by. She jumped off her horse and hid in the trees. As the soldiers neared, they spotted her horse.

"Is that a horse over there?" she heard one of them say.

"It is! It's mine!" she heard the other reply.

"Oh, come on, I spotted it first!" They were close, their voices clear. She heard their feet hit the ground. They grabbed the reins of her horse, and she stepped out.

"I wouldn't do that if I were you. That horse is already claimed." Her voice was stern.

Surprised, they took a step back and drew their swords. "Who are you?" the bigger one said. She just smiled, and before they knew it, she had disarmed both of them and raised her sword to one of their throats.

"That makes no difference. I want to know what's happened here." Neither one answered. She pressed her sword into the one's throat. A thin line of blood ran from the tip of the blade. "Shall I ask again, or do you want to just tell me? I only need one of you alive to tell me." She smiled and pushed the sword a little harder.

"Okay, okay…," the soldier stammered.

She released the pressure. "That's better, now speak."

"Gusta, they attacked us from the south."

Azailia was baffled. Itaear had always been at peace with the surrounding towns, especially Gusta. They had practically been one town.

"Why!" she demanded, her voice almost a scream.

"Well, a little while ago, Reverus called a town meeting. He claimed that he had a spy who had returned with news that Gusta was planning to attack. So he declared an all-hands to build a wall around the city." The guard waved his arm at the wall behind him. "Sure enough, a week or so later, Gusta marched on us. It was a gruesome battle, but we ended up pushing them back."

Her mind raced. It didn't make sense. Why would Gusta attack? There had to be some other reason. Momentarily distracted, the guard pushed Azailia back. "RUN!" he yelled at the other guard. They turned, jumped on their horses and galloped for the town.

Azailia ran to her horse and grabbed her bow. She nocked an arrow, aimed and released. The arrow flew threw the air and hit one guard directly. She grabbed another arrow, but it was too late. The other guard had made it through the gate.

She knew she didn't have much time, so she grabbed their swords and made her way to the pit. She tossed the swords in. "Ignis!" she said, and the entire pit erupted in flames. The flames grew larger, sending dark clouds of smoke into the sky. As she watched the flames grow, bells rang out across the town.

Soldiers poured out of the gates and bounded towards her. She climbed her horse and surged forward. The soldiers were fast, but she could outrun them. She was almost to the top of the hill when an enormous apparition appeared directly in front of her. Her horse reared, knocking her to the ground. She shot up to her feet and prepared for anything, but it was gone. The apparition had disappeared. She grabbed the reins of her horse and patted him. The soldiers arrived and created a half circle around her. Azailia's fingers fidgeted around her hilt, just waiting.

"Clear your mind," she remembered Zeigen saying in a training lesson. It had been a clear day. Zeigen had blindfolded Azailia, and she could hear his voice moving around her as he circled her.

"The point of this exercise is to clear your mind to a point where you can expect any attack." As he stopped talking, a sharp pain shot through Azailia's shoulder as he hit her with the flat of his sword.

"In order to fight, you must have a clear mind so you can sense any change in your surroundings." He struck again. This time, Azailia moved but, again, too late, and she got hit.

"Better," he had said. "I want you to concentrate on everything around me. Put your concentration on the trees, the wind, even on the temperature—everything else but me." Azailia had tried, but a little of her attention remained on Zeigen. The next time, she felt a disruption in the wind to the left of her. She moved to the right. Again, too late; the sword came in contact with her ribs. She fell to the ground as the pain shot through her body. Slowly, she returned to her feet.

"I told you to concentrate on everything but me. You had attention on me, didn't you?" She did not answer. For the next hour, they had practiced this exercise. Her body was continually hit, and bruises had begun to appear all over her body.

"Again!" Zeigen had commanded, his frustration showing. "I know you can do this. Focus!"

She took a deep breath, relaxed her muscles and calmed her mind. She felt the wind blowing through her hair. She felt the trees swaying to the east. She felt the heat on her skin.

She felt the wind violently change directions, and the temperature on her right suddenly dropped. She jumped left and felt something barely miss her ribs. She pulled off the blindfold.

"See! I knew you could do it!" Zeigen had said, pleasantly.

Clear your mind, she remembered again.

Now, being surrounded by soldiers, she took a few deep breaths and relaxed her muscles. Her fingers were resting on the pommel of her sword. She pushed her attention out around her, her eyes resting calmly on the soldiers in front of her.

A soldier from the middle of the crowd stepped out. "By order of Lord Reverus, you are commanded to come with us. If you do not comply, we will use any force necessary." His tone was flat and matter-of-fact.

Using the same flat tone, with her own sarcastic twist, Azailia responded, "I am so sorry, I just won't be able to do that today. Maybe tomorrow."

"I will give you one more chance." His tone was still flat.

"I am sorry, I just can't."

"You leave me no choice. Guards, seize her." Just then, Azailia sensed something. She dodged left as a dagger flew by her. The soldier looked down and coughed, blood spraying from his mouth as he fell to the ground, a dagger protruding from his chest.

Azailia whipped around, and standing about ten feet away from her was the Pravicus. He was dressed in white robes, another small dagger resting in his hand.

"Welcome back, Azailia," he said with a sinister smile. "I am glad you have returned. We were so worried about you," His disgustingly sweet voice made her shiver. "I am so sorry for how rude that soldier was being." He looked past her at the guard lying dead. "I don't think he'll be bothering you anymore though." He made a noise that she thought was a laugh. "Now, will you escort an old man back, please?"

"You're disgusting. I'm not going anywhere with you." She spat. "I haven't forgotten what happened last time." She stared directly in his eyes.

"You little shit." His entire demeanor changed right before her eyes. His eyes darkened, and his smile disappeared. The air around him even seemed to darken. "You're coming with me whether you like it or not. And I don't think your parents are going to save you this time." A knowing smile spread across his face. She flinched and gripped her sword tightly. "Now, why don't you make this easy on both of us? Well, easy on me, painless for you." The same dreadful chuckle escaped once more, amused by his own words.

Azailia didn't respond immediately. Her mind was racing. She knew she couldn't defeat the Pravicus. He was far too powerful, even with her new training. She couldn't outrun them; there were too many. Her mind raced as she searched for some solution.

One of your biggest strengths is that you're smart, she remembered, Zeigen's words coming back to her. He was right. She could figure this out. She just needed a diversion, a way to outsmart them. Then it hit her—the perfect plan. A wry smile spread across her face as she locked eyes with the Pravicus.

"You know what?" she said. The Pravicus tilted his head in curiosity, inviting her to continue. "Fuck. You!"

In one swift motion, she drew her sword and spun down in a crouch. She placed her hand against the ground and cried out, "Appagere." A blinding light burst from the ground, causing her horse to run off. Azailia jumped high in the air as the soldiers and Pravicus took a step back. She looked down to see some of the soldiers scattering, others staying in formation, their weapons pointed at her.

She landed on the ground as the Pravicus lunged at her with great speed. A sword materialized in his hands as he came closer. She quickly deflected his attack. She spun her sword around and brought it down towards the Pravicus. He raised his other hand. Another blade materialized, and he blocked. He brought his other sword around at her. She spun to the left as it went by. Back and forth they fought, neither showing weakness.

She started to tire. The Pravicus was so fast she could barely keep up. He lunged again, bringing his swords down. She brought her sword up just in time to block both. The Pravicus opened his left hand, the sword vanishing. He held his open palm directly in front of her. A surge of energy exploded from it, launching her onto her back.

She lifted her arm, but the Pravicus stepped on her, pinning her to the ground, his other sword pressed to her throat.

"In what world did you think you could beat me? You're pitiful." He looked up at the soldiers. "Well? What are you waiting for? Come get her." The soldiers rushed over. They grabbed her underneath both her arms and dragged her back to town.

The soldiers threw her on the same table as before and strapped her down. The Pravicus glided over, his creepy smile back. He pulled a dagger from inside his robes.

"Do you know what this is?" he asked as he ran the blade over her skin. The dagger was black with a dark jewel in the pommel. It exuded evil; Azailia could even see a black aura coming off it. "Of course you don't. It was made with very dark magic. When it takes someone's life, it absorbs their spirit." He moved behind her head, "They call it 'Salareif', which literally means 'Soul Reaper'." And he plunged the dagger into her heart. An animalistic scream was heard ringing throughout.

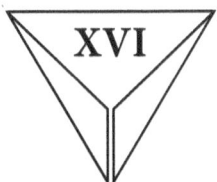

XVI

In one swift motion, she drew her sword and spun down in a crouch. She placed her hand against the ground and cried out, "Appagere." A blinding light burst from the ground. Using the cover of the light, she jumped on her horse, hanging herself off the side opposite the Pravicus. Her horse bounded away from the commotion.

When she was a little ways away, she slid onto the saddle and turned to see her apparition fighting with the Pravicus. She smiled as she turned and continued to ride hard until the town was out of sight.

It was time to get back on track, she thought. She turned north, headed towards the Jetra River. That's where she saw the man lying in her vision. She rode for a long time, her body way more exhausted than she had expected. The spell had really drained her.

As the sun started to set, she figured it was a good time to stop for the night. She didn't want to camp anywhere open. She had to find something more secluded. Ahead of her on the left, she spotted a rock formation on top of a hill. It was a perfectly hidden spot to rest for the night. It seemed the rocks were almost arranged in a circle. She jumped off her horse before getting too close and drew her sword. She crept closer with her sword hidden. There was no sound as she came up on the rocks. She went all the way around them, and when she was satisfied it was clear, she went back and walked her horse over.

She found a nice spot where she could lie down and her horse could graze. She grabbed a few blankets and pulled out some food she had packed. She ate the food quickly, feeling instantly better.

"So what are we going to call you?" she said to the horse. The horse continued to eat. "Well I think you definitely deserve a name. Let me think...." She thought of his ability to maneuver through the forest and his bravery earlier that day. "You deserve something strong." She patted him on his nose, feeling his soft skin.

"How about Marv?" The horse didn't move, just kept eating. "Okay, no. How about Augustus?" The horse snorted. "Yeah, I agree. That doesn't suit you." She lay down.

"I know. How about Prow?" He moved his muzzle over to her and licked her face. "I love it! It's the perfect name too. In the old language, it means 'valiant and brave'. Suits you perfectly." She yawned. "Goodnight, Prow." And she fell asleep.

It only seemed like a few minutes had gone by before the sun was trying to burst through her eyelids. She opened her eyes and looked around. Everything was quiet. Prow stood next to her, grazing. Azailia stood up and pulled out a little more food and ate it.

Next, she pulled out a piece of parchment and laid it out on the rock. She had been using this to create a map. She grabbed a small quill and a vial of ink. She added the rock formation to the map. Currently, she had the Mintual Forest, Itaear, Gusta and part of the Jetra River. She hadn't added the Drutas camp in case someone got a hold of the map. When the ink had dried, she rolled up the map and put everything back.

Once all was packed, she mounted Prow and continued north.

Later that day, she entered the Mintual Forest again. The forest curved east quite a bit from where she originally exited. From other maps she had seen, this was the most direct route to the Jetra River. This part of the forest was very different than the area closer to the Drutas camp entrance.

As she made her way through, she noticed a lot of the trees had been cut down. Stumps covered the ground. The forest wasn't nearly as lush either. Dead leaves littered the surface. A weird feeling crept into her body, and she urged Prow faster. Something was off here, and she wanted to get out quickly.

She exited the forest just after nightfall. It was a hard ride, but because the forest was so open, she was able to move fast. She found a secluded place and camped for the night, exhaustion taking over.

The next morning, she was woken by a loud rushing noise. It sounded like the wind had picked up dramatically and was pushing the trees violently together. She opened her eyes and stretched. Realizing there was no wind, she looked around but couldn't find the source of the noise. That's when it dawned on her. The River! It was close.

She ate her food, updated her map, packed everything and, in no time, was racing towards the noise. The river came into view shortly after. She had never seen it and was astounded. It was massive in width, and it stretched endlessly. It was beautiful. She took a moment to take in the view, allowing Prow some time to quench his thirst.

Coming back to her senses, she remembered the

man. She needed to find him, but how? The river was much bigger than she had originally thought. The idea seemed impossible.

Calm yourself and focus, Zeigen's voice said in her mind.

She sat down on the riverbank and closed her eyes. Once again, she relaxed her muscles. She pushed her attention out. She felt all the tiny particles of water running around the rocks. She could sense the uncontrollable fear of the fish as they tried to swim upstream; she even felt Prow's exhaustion as he grazed calmly beside her.

She pushed her attention further and felt the wind blowing against the birds in the sky. She felt the trees dancing in the wind as it pushed them back and forth. She turned her attention more towards the river. She didn't find anything unusual. She pushed farther upstream. The river became much wider farther north. Rocks became a lot more abundant and the rapids harsh.

Then she sensed it. The void, it was there in the rocks. She pushed hard, focusing on that spot. It began to form the more she concentrated, and there he was. His body lay tangled in a group of rocks.

Her eyes snapped open, she leaped on Prow and together they darted forward. She sped along the river, keeping her eyes open for the rock formation. She saw it up ahead and skidded to a halt. She scanned the rocks, looking for anything that resembled a body. There it was; resting over one of the rocks was an arm. Jumping off of Prow, she unhooked her sword, letting it fall to the ground, and dove into the water. Using the rocks to brace herself, she maneuvered to the body. She could definitely see that it was a person. He was unconscious and looked extremely worn down. When she was near him, she threw his arm over her shoulder and, using every ounce of strength she had, pulled them back to the edge. She got him out of the river and collapsed next to him, breathing heavily.

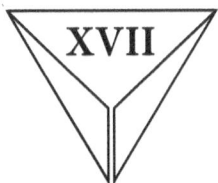

XVII

Catching her breath, she sat up and looked down. Now that she could really see him, she realized he was just a boy, probably close to her own age. He was fairly tall and had shaggy blonde hair. His body was extremely worn down; it looked as if he had been in the water for weeks. His clothes were ragged, and he had two burn marks on each side of his temples.

She checked his pulse and could feel his heart beating, but it was very faint. He was still breathing, but he was barely hanging on. Using most of her strength, she hoisted him up onto Prow. She carefully slid behind him so he was draped in front of her. She made a few clicking noises and nudged Prow forward.

They traveled slower than she wanted, but she didn't want to chance harming the boy any more than he already was. It took her almost three days to arrive back to the hidden entrance of the camp. She had not run into anyone as she had on her first trip to the camp. She reached the wall where her parents and her had entered a while back, but then she realized she had no way of getting in.

She jumped down and examined the wall. The grass was extremely green near the opening but there was no evidence of footprints. Even as she walked, her footsteps disappeared behind her. She realized an enchantment must have been cast so no traces were left. She walked back and forth around the general location of the entrance.

"HELLO!" she screamed. No answer. She banged on the wall, tried spells, even screamed multiple times, but nothing changed. She leaned against the wall and sunk down, bringing her knees to her chest.

"Why can't I get in?" she said, almost crying the words. The pressure of everything caved in on her. What happened to her normal life in Itaear? She missed the soft bed and quiet nights. She missed the friendly people and Rose. She missed her best friend. Everything was so much more peaceful back then. She put her hands over her face, the tears flowing freely now.

"Why. Is. Nothing. Working?" she screamed aloud. For a few minutes, she just let the despair overcome her.

"Okay. I can do this," she told herself. "I am stronger than this. Zeigen would be so disappointed if he saw me right now," she said, trying to give herself some encouragement. She pulled herself off the ground, rubbed her eyes dry and looked around.

"The wall is not opening." She paused. "Well, thanks, captain obvious," she said to herself and laughed. Her mood lifted a little bit. She looked up in the sky, and it was getting dark; clouds had started to appear. *Crap,* she thought. Preparing for rain, she grabbed the blankets from her bag and strung them up between trees. She moved the boy off the horse and under the blankets. She made a small fire as much under the shelter as she could.

The night went on forever. The trees were restless in the wind. The later it got, the more the wind picked up, and sure enough rain started to fall. Time dragged by, but she wasn't sure how late, or early, it was. The constant rain had long since put out the fire. She pulled her legs in close, trying to keep warm.

Finally, the rain stopped, the clouds parted and the moon came out. She stood up and stretched, her body stiff from the cold. She checked the boy. He was dry and moderately warm. He was still breathing, but it was slow, and her concern returned.

She looked up at the moon. It was huge and created so much light. Azailia could see perfectly. The night air was crisp; it was that unique air just after a spring rain. The sun had just gone down, so there was a faint glow on the horizon. The owls had come out and started their nightly hunt.

The beauty brought her back to a time when Azailia was only about eight years old. She had just been given her first training lesson from her father. It was tiring, so her muscles were all tense. She really had not cared too much about training. She just wanted to play and have fun, but her father had insisted.

She blinked her eyes and smiled. The memory reminded her of simpler times. The grass was crisp, and the sky was clear back then. There was no magic, no Drutas or Pravicus. She sighed then stood up and walked back over to the boy. She found a moderately dry spot to lie down and closed her eyes.

Azailia woke up just as the sun was peering over the horizon. A faint glow illuminated the forest. The sun danced off the water that had accumulated on the leaves. She stood up and stretched. She checked the boy again, and he was still in the same condition. She looked at the wall, sighed and grabbed some food from her bag.

Once again, she tried to open the door. She tried more phrases in the old language but still nothing. She started pacing in front of the wall and racked her brain for anything she could think of. Nothing new came to her.

As she paced, she noticed the shadows of the trees. Instead of receding as they should, they were growing. She thought her mind was playing tricks on her, but, sure enough, the shadows were growing, and towards her. She reached out, the shadows engulfing her hand. That's when she felt it—emptiness. It was like a black hollowness had grown inside of her, and she felt dead. She immediately pulled her hand back, a slight burning sensation flaring up. She knew she had to get away from the shadows.

She ran to the boy and heaved him onto Prow. Prow even seemed to feel it; he was fidgeting nervously. She jumped on and turned to lead them out, but the shadows had blocked her way. She turned Prow to the left and shot forward but then stopped. The shadows had that way blocked also. She turned to go the other way but to no avail. They were growing closer and closer, boxing them in.

They were backed up to the wall when she heard a cracking noise. She turned to see the wall opening. Relief spread through her as it opened fully, and they shot through, the shadows just closing in. As they bounded into the camp, she took one last look and saw a long, decayed hand reaching out for her. The wall closed, and it was gone.

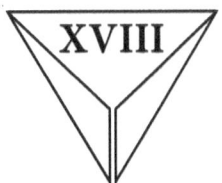

XVIII

Everything moved at an accelerated pace. Before she knew it, arms were grabbing her, helping her down. Another set of arms were carrying the boy down. She reached out.

"He needs help," she choked out, her eyes blurring. She heard a marching noise and turned to see a group of soldiers marching to the wall. It had reopened. "What's going on?" she said hazily, still overwhelmed by all the commotion. The arms released her. She saw that one them was Zeigen's, but she didn't recognize the others. "Zeigen!" She shouted louder than she meant to, but she was so relieved. He smiled at her.

"Where are they taking him?" She pointed to the men carrying the boy away. As she did, her vision blurred and her knees gave out. She could feel Zeigen catch her.

"Vaidya!" she heard Zeigen call out. A woman rushed over, grabbed Azailia's chin and looked at her.

"This way!" she commanded, intensity in her voice. Zeigen and another man carried Azailia after the lady. She turned back. "Did the," this question directed at Azailia, "shadows touch you?" Azailia's head lolled to the left. She tried to speak, but her mouth wouldn't move. Her vision continued to fade out. "Did … the … shadows

... touch ... you?" The voice seemed so far. It felt like the lady was miles away. She tried to focus on the words, but everything went dark.

Azailia awoke in a small bed. A small blanket covered her. She opened her eyes and looked around. The room was very small. By the foot of the bed stood a small cabinet, a candle lit on top; to her left, a chair with Zeigen sitting in it. As soon as he saw her eyes open, he stood up and walked over.

"You're awake. How are you feeling?" He turned to look behind him. "Vaidya!" he shouted. The lady came rushing in a second later. She was wearing a white apron that was stained red. She pushed Zeigen out of the way and bent down over Azailia. She examined Azailia's eyes, pressed her fingers on the sides of her throat, pressed on her stomach and then picked up Azailia's hand. She flipped it over, examining both sides.

Azailia tried to sit up. Halfway up, her head went light, and she started to fall back down.

"Whoa there," Vaidya said calmly as she helped her lay back down. "You need to take it easy. The Arrach did more damage than we thought. Luckily for you, we were here." She gave Azailia a genuine smile.

"The *Arrach*?" she stammered.

"Shh ... wait until you have more strength." She pushed a cup of steaming liquid in front of Azailia's face. The smell was awful, and she turned away.

"Come on now. I know it smells bad, but it'll keep you alive. Trust me, it tastes better than it smells." Vaidya moved the cup in front of her again. Azailia held her breath and took a sip cautiously. The taste exploded in her mouth. It tasted amazing! It was like biting into a fresh strawberry. She gulped it down.

"There you go. I told you." She smiled, taking the cup away. "Now you sleep and we'll return later." Azailia had already been fading and was out before she had finished her sentence.

She woke up again to find that Zeigen had brought some chicken broth for her to drink. She drank it slowly followed by the delicious, bad smelling tea and fell back asleep. Azailia wasn't sure how long this went on—she assumed a few days, but everything ran together.

One morning when she woke up, no one was in the room with her. She looked around, and it still looked the same. She pushed herself up noticing she felt much better. She didn't get lightheaded at all; in fact, she felt strong again. When she was sitting up, she noticed her hand ached. She looked at it and saw the remnants of black lines on her fingers.

Zeigen walked in just then and saw her sitting up. He smiled, "Good to see you're awake! How do you feel?"

"Good," she said, her voice cracking slightly. She hadn't spoken in a while, and her throat was dry.

Zeigen handed her a cup of water. "You probably need this." She gulped it down. "Vaidya," he called as she finished the water. Vaidya walked in a few minutes later and sat down.

"How are you feeling?" she said as she looked Azailia up and down.

"Actually, quite good. How long have I been out?" Azailia replied, taking another sip of water.

"About two weeks." Azailia coughed into the cup.

"Two weeks?" she choked out. Vaidya nodded.

"I'll let Zeigen explain everything. I just wanted to make sure you were doing okay. When you feel strong enough, you're free to go." She stood to leave.

"Wait." She held her hand up to Vaidya. "What are these?" she asked, indicating the black lines on her arm.

"Those," she frowned, "are the marks of an Arrach. Don't worry; they'll go away. But had you not been treated immediately, it would have killed you. Now, I have others I need to attend to. Zeigen will answer any more of your questions. I'm glad you're feeling better." With that, she departed.

Zeigen looked her up and down, the worry that had been on his face replaced with relief. "I'm sure you're hungry. I brought you some solid food." He set a plate of fruits and vegetables next to her.

She barely noticed. Her mind was racing with all the questions she had. "What's an Arrach?"

"Well," he began as he sat down in the chair, "there's not much we know about them. People call them Shadow Demons, Reapers, but we know them as Arrachs. From what we've learned, they were created from Dark Magic, using pure dark energy. Someone has to be very strong and use a lot of dark energy to be able to summon and control them."

Azailia shivered as she remembered the skeleton-like hand reaching out for her. "If they stay in the shadows, why did I see a skeletal hand?"

"They kill in two different ways. The first is through the poison that you just experienced. Fortunately for you, we were able to treat you before the worst could occur. When you came in contact with the shadow of the Arrach, you probably noticed the empty feeling that spread through you?" She nodded, not wanting to remember that awful sensation. "That is poison. It seeps through your entire body, absorbing every bit of life force you have. The point is to paralyze you. If not treated immediately, and somehow you get away, you would experience the most excruciating pain you've ever felt until you finally die." He paused, his face darkening as if remembering a horrible experience.

"The second way they kill is, once you're paralyzed, they reveal themselves from the shadows. They are then able to stab you in the heart using a dagger, which they call 'Salareif'. This dagger absorbs your life force and feeds the Arrach. It's another very painful death but not as bad as dying from their poison." He stopped. His eyes had gone dark again and stared blankly past her.

"Are you okay?" There was concern in her voice as she looked at him.

"Yeah," he said, but she could tell something was off. Something told her that he had experience with these creatures.

"What was that delicious tea?" she asked, hoping to change the subject. His eyes regained focus, and a smile returned to his face.

"Oh, it's good, isn't it? Once you get past the smell that is." He chuckled. "It's called 'Mederi'. What did it taste like to you?"

"Fresh strawberries," she said, confused. "It tastes different to everyone?"

"Yep. For me, it tasted like fresh bacon." He smacked his lips like he could taste it again.

"Wait, you've been poisoned by an Arrach?"

"Let's save that story for another time. How about that?" he said with a tone that told her not to press on. "So, do you want to—"

"THE BOY! Where is he? Is he alive?" Azailia interrupted, the boy popping into her head.

"Don't worry, he's alive. He's still unconscious but is stable. Want to see him?"

"Absolutely!"

They left the little room and walked across the field, headed towards the training field. Azailia had been staying in a building behind the Torr. Zeigen led her into the forest to a very large tree with vines covering the entire base. The tree was massive—the size of a small hut. Zeigen walked right up to the center of the tree. He reached his hand out, said a word in the old language and backed up. The vines wiggled alive, starting to spread out and retract. Before long, an opening had appeared, and they walked through.

Inside was a single room. Lying on the bed in the back was the boy. He was still unconscious. The room looked very similar to the one she had been in—just about the same size with a small cabinet and a single chair. A water basin sat atop the cabinet. There was no candle; the room was lit by openings very far above her. She realized she was inside the tree. The light came from the sun.

"Amazing!" she said, awestruck as she watched the entrance close. She turned her attention to the boy lying on the bed. He looked so peaceful. The color in his face had returned, and his breathing seemed steady. She heard the vines cracking and turned to see Vaidya walking in. She smiled as she passed Azailia. She grabbed a washcloth and went to sit beside him.

"How's he doing?" Azailia asked her as she dabbed the boy's forehead.

"He's okay—stable at least. He's been like this for a while now," she replied as she set the cloth down and checked his pulse.

"What happened to him?"

"We're not sure. All we know is he's lucky to be alive. He would be dead for sure if you hadn't found him when you did." She tore two pieces of cloth and dipped them in a salve she had produced. There was a piece of cloth on each side of his temple. She replaced them with the new pieces.

"What's that?" Azailia asked curiously.

"They are severe burn marks. Not sure where they came from, but they're almost healed now. I've never seen anything like it. I don't know what would cause something like that." Azailia moved in to get a closer look. Fear struck her as she looked at the burn marks. She had seen them before; in fact, she had even seen how they were made. She shuffled back away from the boy. Zeigen and Vaidya both looked at her, concerned.

"What? Do you know what caused them?" Zeigen asked, his face now serious.

"More than that. I have seen it done!" she stammered. This got their attention. "Before I left my town, before coming here, when the Pravicus first arrived. I knew something was wrong with them. I went to see Reverus, the Lord of Itaear. I heard a commotion, so I crept around the side, and I saw him strapped down on a table. The Pravicus was holding his hands at the side of Reverus' temples. Energy was shooting into his head." She looked at Zeigen, "He wasn't the same after that. He was more docile. He did everything the Pravicus said." Zeigen left the room hurriedly. Vaidya even slid a little away from the boy.

Azailia looked over the boy. He didn't look evil. But then again, some of the most evil people in the world can fool you. Zeigen returned shortly with two guards.

"You two do not leave this room. Understood?" Zeigen commanded.

"Yes Sir," they both responded.

"If he wakes up, alert me immediately." The guards nodded. "Azailia, let's go. I need you to tell me everything."

She told Zeigen everything that had happened, from before she left Itaear, to her adventure of finding the boy. He listened intently, just nodding as she recalled the tale. When she was done, he sent her to rest.

A few days went by. Each day, she would go visit the boy. The two guards, and occasionally Vaidya, would greet her, but there was never anything new with the boy.

One day, she was sitting in the fields with Zeigen. "One thing I don't understand," she said as she looked out over the fields, "why didn't the door open for me? I tried everything."

Zeigen turned his gaze on her. "The door, as you know, is enchanted. Only a few people can open that door. Remember those men who greeted you when you first arrived in the forest?"

"You mean the ones that blended into the forest?" she said, recalling how stunned she was that they could simply disappear.

"Yes. They are called the Guardians. They guard the door and alert us if anyone threatens or, in your case, needs to enter."

"Okay...," Azailia said, confused. "Where were they? I was out there forever."

"We weren't sure, until," he paused as if the memory pained him, "a patrol had returned after we brought you in. They had found the bodies of all the Guardians. The Arrach had drained them all."

They sat together for a while after that, silent. As it got late, the air cooled around them. They were getting up to leave when a guard came rushing up to them.

"Sir," he said, out of breath.

"What is it?"

"It's the boy, Sir. He's awake!"

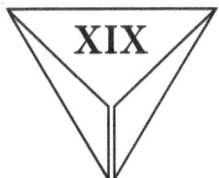

XIX

The boy opened his eyes and looked around. He was in a very plain room. At the foot of the bed was a small cabinet with a basin on top. Beside the door stood a single guard staring at him intently.

"You're awake," Vaidya said, her voice strained. She was sitting in the chair beside his bed. "How do you feel?"

"Where am I?" he said. His throat ached as he spoke. She didn't respond, just handed him a cup of water. He tried to gulp it down and immediately coughed it back up. The water burned.

"Slow," she said. "You haven't drunk anything in a while." He followed her direction and took small sips. "Good," she said as he drank. "What's your name?"

The boy thought for a moment. He couldn't remember his name. He furrowed his brow, trying to remember.

"I don't know," he said finally.

"That's okay," she said. "My name is Vaidya. I've been taking care of you." There was a loud cracking noise as the door started to unfold. It looked like a bunch of snakes slithering backwards. A door appeared and two figures walked in.

The first was a man. He was tall and lean but muscular. His dark hair was short, and his face was set with determination. The other was a young girl. She was beautiful. She had long blonde hair and piercing blue eyes. She was thin but not fragile looking.

"Has he said anything?" the man directed at Vaidya.

"No, he doesn't remember his name," she answered.

The man now looked at the boy, "Who are you?"

"Like she said, I don't—"

"Think!" he interrupted, the man's frustration exploding to the surface. The boy shifted his weight, a little taken aback.

"Zeigen!" Vaidya stood up. "You need to take a minute and cool off. He doesn't remember." She pushed him out of the room, the strange slithering doors opening again. The beautiful girl remained, her eyes soft as she looked over him. He felt like he knew her. She seemed so familiar. No matter how hard he tried, he couldn't remember. Vaidya sat back down, pulling his attention back to her.

"Sorry about him. He's not angry with you. He's got a lot of other things going on." She sounded apologetic. "Can you remember anything?"

Again, he tried to think of something, anything that felt familiar. He tried to remember his parents—nothing. He tried to remember where he came from or how he got here. Nothing. He shook his head, frustrated.

"Nothing. It's all blank. It's like I didn't exist before today. But that can't be true." It frustrated him that he couldn't remember. Vaidya looked at him with a mix of pity and understanding.

The girl moved closer to his bed. "My name is Azailia." Her voice was sweet but nervous. "I'm the one who found you and brought you here."

"Found me? Found me where?" the boy said blankly.

"You were caught on some rocks in the Jetra." She paused, noticing the puzzled look on his face. "The river? You don't even remember that?" He shook his head. "Okay," her face softened, "the Jetra is the largest river in NeaVall. I found you in it. You were unconscious, wedged between some rocks."

He thought for a moment then shook his head again. "I just don't remember."

"Okay," Vaidya said before Azailia could continue. "I think that's enough for today. You need to rest. We'll come back tomorrow."

"Both of you?" he asked quietly, glancing at Azailia.

"Yes," Azailia answered with a smile as they left.

The next few days went by quickly. The boy continued to gain his strength back. His boney physique had been replaced by lean muscle. He had shaved and cut his hair, accentuating his natural features. His appetite had become enormous. He would sometimes eat six full meals in one day. Every day, he worked with Vaidya to try to recover his memories. The best part of his day though was when Azailia would come visit. She had convinced Zeigen to allow her to take him on walks. His only condition was that two guards accompany them. The boy still had trouble remembering anything. He began getting flashes but never a solid memory. He just enjoyed listening to Azailia tell stories.

"River!" Azailia yelled to him as she jogged up to him. They had been calling him River since he couldn't remember his name. It seemed to fit. A guard stood next to him; it was the only way he was allowed to leave his hut.

As Azailia approached him, a smile broke across his face. He always loved looking at her—the way her hair glistened in the sunlight; the sound of her voice; even simply being next to her made him feel lighter.

"Good news!" she said between breaths. "We may have found a way to get your memories back." River's mood immediately shifted. This was great news. It had been days since he had even had a flashback.

"Really! How?" he said, his excitement immediately apparent.

"Zeigen has been doing some research since you arrived. He learned of a technique called "Mimara". He didn't explain much to me, just sent me to come get you."

"Let's get moving then!" River said impatiently.

They found Zeigen in a part of the forest devoid of trees. The open field was not too large—probably large enough for fifty people to comfortably stand. It was in the shape of a rectangle. Along the sides were columns leading to the end of the area. In the back was a statue of a dragon.

Zeigen stood in front of the statue, looking up at it. "Do you know who this is?" His question was directed at both of them. He looked at Azailia, and she looked just as confused as the boy felt.

"No Sir," she said for the both of them. Zeigen turned to face them.

"A long time ago … Azailia, you know this story, and River, you probably do too, just can't remember it. Anyway, a long time ago, we actually lived with dragons. The dragons had become fed up with man and his pettiness. They devised a plan to take with them Thirteen Chosen. When the Thirteen returned, they were supposed to use the knowledge they learned to educate man and when their task was complete, the dragons would return.

"However, when the Thirteen returned, the king had

other plans. During their absence, the king had devised a plan to kill the Thirteen and rule the way he saw fit. But before he could follow through with it, the Thirteenth learned of his plan and escaped. The king framed him for the murders of the other twelve, turning the world against him.

"This statue is in honor of the dragon who chose the Thirteenth."

"I always hear them referred to as their number. Do they have real names?" Azailia asked.

"They did, but when they were chosen, their names were forgotten. To be chosen was a great honor. To be called the number was a sign of respect." He looked backed at the statue one more time and turned to them. "Anyway, the reason I called you two here—I'm sure Azailia told you that we found a possible way to recall your past memories?" He addressed River.

"Yes. I think she said it was called 'Mimara'? What is that?"

"It's a very old technique where one can recall memories. Usually, it's used to remember a specific detail, not a full memory, but it may work in this case too." He looked past the two. "Kohen, good timing. I was just explaining the technique."

A man walked up behind them. His appearance was non-threatening. His hair was short, his build was average and his eyes were kind. He wore a robe with a sash around the waist. He reminded River of a monk. Kohen walked up and bowed to the three.

"It's weird," River said, "as you were walking up, I thought you resembled a monk. But, I can't remember ever meeting a monk. I just know the idea of what a monk is. Is that good?"

Kohen thought about it for a moment. "Any type of recall is good. It means your mind is still working. It probably just needs some repairs. I can help you with that." His voice was soft and friendly. He then turned to Zeigen. "If you don't mind, I would like to get started."

"Of course." Zeigen turned to Azailia. "Let's go. River, I'll send Azailia to get you later."

When the two had left, Kohen sat down and indicated for River to do the same. "As you were told, this technique is called Mimara. What we'll do is strengthen your mind. Doing this should release your memories. I heard you've been having flashes of memory. Tell me about one."

River closed his eyes and thought. He picked one. "I was a boy. I look six. I was trying to help my father cut wood, but I couldn't lift the axe." River opened his eyes. "That's all I remember."

"Good," Kohen said, no other indication in his face. "Go over it again."

River closed his eyes again. "I was a boy. I was six. I was trying to help my father cut wood, but I couldn't lift the axe. He laughs and pats me on the back. He's wearing dark pants and a light shirt. It's hot outside."

River continued to recall more and more as he continued to go over it in his mind. As he went over it the seventh time, his eyes shot open.

"I remember the entire thing! It's a perfect memory!"

"Excellent!" Kohen said. "Tell me the whole thing." River did so.

They did this every day. Kohen would have him pick flashes of memories that would come back to him, and they would go over them again and again. Each time, the full memory would snap back. Some took longer than others, but, without fail, the memory would return.

When Azailia would come get him at the end of the day, he would recount the memories he had recalled that day. Each day, she would ask him if he had recalled his name, but he still hadn't remembered it.

As the days went, Zeigen would get reports. He thought it acceptable to move him into the main berthing. Azailia's parents had yet to return, so she had offered to look after him.

River fell asleep quickly on the sixth night. He had recalled four memories that day. The exercise always left him drained, and Kohen was very strict on him getting enough sleep. His mind was restless. Flashes of a new memory came to him. He tossed in his sleep violently.

He saw a white cloak, followed by a man convulsing as energy surged through his head. There was an evil laughter that echoed in his head. Then he was crouching on a roof, looking down.

"River...." He heard a voice.

Someone grabbed his shoulder. He turned but couldn't make out the person.

"River...," the voice said again.

The person wouldn't let go. He fought against the person holding his shoulder.

"River ... wake up!"

He grabbed the person's arm and pushed back with all his strength. He had to get free.

"RIVER!"

His eyes snapped open. Azailia stood over him, her hand on his shoulder. Her face was barely illuminated by the single candle in the room, but he could see the worry on her face. He sat up as she removed her arm and rubbed it. He noticed scratches and red marks all over her arm. He rubbed his left arm. It tingled from laying on it.

157

"You were screaming in your sleep. Are you okay?" The concern in her voice was noticeable.

"Did I do that?" he said, not paying attention, feeling regret and shame.

"It's not bad. Are you okay?" He nodded, still shaken up.

"Okay good." She got up to leave, but River grabbed her wrist. She turned.

"Will you stay with me?" he whispered. She turned and nodded. He scooted back, and she lay down in front of him. She pressed her back to his chest. "Thank you," he whispered as he fell back asleep, his arm draped around her waist.

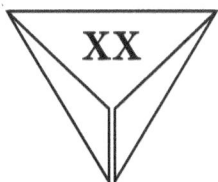

XX

River awoke the next morning to find that Azailia was already gone. He sat up and placed his feet on the floor. The night had definitely taken it out of him. He had only gotten to sleep fully when Azailia had laid down with him. A small smile came across his face as he remembered the warmth of her body pressed against his—the way her body fit into his. Even her smell was pleasing to him.

He stood up and stretched. He had to meet with Kohen today. As much as he didn't want to, he knew he had to go over the flash of memory he had last night. After dressing, he made his way to the mess hall for some food. He scanned the room and didn't see Azailia. He was disappointed but knew he would see her later. He quickly ate and made his way to his normal meeting spot.

Zeigen stood there with Kohen. They were arguing.

"Not until we know for sure!" Zeigen was saying as River walked up.

"It would be good for him! It may help the process! We're making so much progress," Kohen responded.

Zeigen saw River walk up. "Not until we know. That's final!" And he walked off.

"What was that about, Kohen?" River asked as Zeigen disappeared back to town.

"Nothing, really. He doesn't think we're making fast enough progress, and I suggested Azailia train you." River brightened up at the thought of that. "He doesn't think it's a good idea. He still doesn't trust you fully."

"But why? I could use the extra exercises," River protested, knowing Kohen couldn't change anything.

"That's what I thought, but he said no. That's that." River kicked the ground in disappointment. "We can let it get us down or work harder. Azailia found me this morning, said you had a bad dream. How did she know, eh?" He smiled knowingly as he nudged River in the side. River smiled and together they walked over to where they had been working.

"Did you eat this morning?" Kohen said as they sat facing each other. River nodded. "Okay, good. Tell me about this dream."

River closed his eyes. "I remember a man in a white robe. He was hovering over another man. I remember the man was biting into a piece of wood. He was convulsing. I remember laughter. I remember looking down." He opened his eyes.

"Good!" Kohen said. "Again."

River closed his eyes again. "I remember looking down through an opening. I was crouched. I was looking down at the man in the white robe. The man on the table was convulsing."

"Good. Again."

Back and forth they went. River kept remembering more and more details, but he couldn't release the full memory. There was one part that he just couldn't recall.

"Good," Kohen said, as River completed recalling it for the twentieth time. "Let's take a break."

Frustrated, River agreed, and Kohen sent him to get

food. It was past the time where food would be available in the mess hall. Most of the time, he would eat with Kohen in between memories. As it was too late, he wandered into town. He had never been there; Zeigen had wanted him to stay away from the majority of people. As he walked through, he realized how many people actually lived in the camp. He also now understood why Zeigen had told him to stay out of the main areas. Everyone stared at him. He was a new face.

He escaped the curious glances by entering a small tavern on his left. It was a hole-in-the-wall place; it didn't even have a name, but he could smell the food. Inside was very small—only a few tables and a bar. There was one man in the place. He was sitting at one of the tables, his head down. He looked up at River as the door closed, his face was sullen.

"Whatcha lookin' for boy?" the gruff looking man said flatly.

"Sorry sir, I was just trying to find some food. Is that delicious smell coming from in here?" River sniffed the air. It was definitely coming from there.

"We're closed," he said. River sighed, his stomach grumbling. He turned to leave. "Wait." The man got up and walked behind the counter. "Have a seat." He motioned to the stools in front of the bar. River walked over and sat down. The man left and returned with a bowl of steaming stew. It smelled incredible.

"So what's y'ur name, boy?" the gruff man asked while River dug into the stew.

"Ri … ver," he said between mouthfuls. The food was delicious. Flavors danced off his tongue with each bite. "Well, actually, I don't know my real name. River is what they call me," he said after he swallowed a big bite.

"Hrmmph." The man grunted. "My name's Nix." He held out his hand and River shook it. He had a handshake that could bring a giant to his knees. River shook his own hand to try to ease the tension when Nix finally let go. Nix let out a hearty laugh. He was a stocky man with a long black beard and hair to match. Nix seemed to relax as his eyes went from cold to a welcoming interest. "So tell me your story, Ri ... ver," he mocked with another chuckle. All River could do was laugh with him.

"Well, I don't remember much. I'm getting my memories back slowly. But from what I'm told, I was found floating in the Jetra River, left for dead. That's why they call me River." He smiled. "Azailia brought me back here, and that's where we're at." Nix just smiled.

"That's a good story, Riv. That Azailia, she's a pretty lass, isn't she." It wasn't a question, more of an assumption. River blushed, a smile spreading across his face. "Ahhhh...." Nix observed. "You two ... eh ... got something going?" River just smiled. "Ha-HA!" Another hearty laugh. "So then what's got-cha down?"

River sunk low, taking another bite. "I'm stuck. My memory isn't coming back, and the one I'm working on won't release." He slammed his fist down on the bar.

"Whoa there, boy," Nix said as he grabbed a glass and wiped it down. "Listen here. All you need to do is relax. You've made impressive progress. Sounds like you're focusing on the one thing that hasn't gone your way. You're alive. You're safe. You even have some of your memories back. Not to mention sounds like you have a beautiful girl." He winked and jerked his head towards the door.

"RIVER!" He heard his name and turned. Azailia stood in the doorway, hands on hips, glaring at him.

"Kohen and I have been looking for you everywhere. He's waiting for you."

"Well, I guess it's time to go. It was good talking to you, and thanks for the food," River said.

"Hey boy," Nix said just as he was leaving, "just remember, sometimes things happen when you're not paying attention." He smiled and closed the door.

Azailia walked with a tone. She was rigid and moved with purpose. River ran to catch up with her and grabbed her arm. She spun, "I can't believe you! You can't just disappear like that." Her voice was strained.

"I know, I'm sorry. I just went to find food," he said calmly. He took her hands in his.

"I came to find you in the field, and Kohen said he sent you for food. I went to look and you weren't there. The guard that was supposed to be with you didn't know where you were either," she replied, her whole body shaking uncontrollably.

"I'm fine. I'm right here." He lifted her chin up with his hand and looked in her eyes. They were sparkling, a mix of tears and the sun reflecting off their deep blue color.

"Kohen was worried." A slight laugh escaped as a smile spread across her face. He couldn't help but smile back. He was lost in her eyes; the rest of the world seemed to fall away. She looked back at him with a yearning he hadn't seen before, her eyes completely focused on his. He started to lean in.

An explosion erupted from the training grounds, pulling their attention. They looked back at each other, the moment gone, and ran towards the training fields. They arrived to see smoke clearing. Two people lay on the ground while others were rushing around.

Zeigen walked out of the smoke, saw them and walked up to them.

"Don't worry," he said, seeing the concern on their faces. "They were practicing a spell, and Fen," he jerked his thumb to a guy standing up, "got a little over-zealous and, well, you can see."

"Oh good, we heard it from town," Azailia said with relief. "We have to go, Kohen is waiting for him." Zeigen nodded and headed back to the commotion.

They turned to go to where Kohen would be, when River spotted a couple of soldiers practicing some spells. They were sitting at a table with a piece of wood in front of them. They were holding their hands over it, and energy was surging into the wood. River looked a little closer when one finished and saw a burn mark on the wood. It looked just like … his mind flashed.

He was somewhere else, back in the Capitol.

"Are you okay to go from here?" Kilas turned and looked at River.

"Yeah, I think so." River just wanted to get away from everyone and collect his thoughts. This was perfect.

"Okay good. Mert is receiving his special training today too, so he'll go with you. Be quick, though; they're expecting you. To make up for the mistake, I made sure they put you in front of the line as soon as you show up."

Damn, River thought. "Okay, we'll head right there," River said, trying to fake enthusiasm. Kilas smiled, clearly waiting for them to leave. Mert and River started towards the training building.

On their way there, Mert was nonstop. He kept talking and talking about how excited he was. River, lost in his own thoughts, just kept absently acknowledging him. As they neared the building, River turned to Mert. "I forgot something back at the barracks. Go on without me. I won't be long." Mert started to protest, but River was already running back.

When he was far enough that no one was paying attention, he doubled back and sneaked around the side of the building. It was time to figure out what was going on in this place.

He moved quietly to the back of the building and found a way to scale the wall. He climbed to the top and onto the roof. Sure enough, there was an opening in the roof. He walked over to it and looked in. River went pale. What he saw was appalling. There, strapped down on the table, was Mert. Hovering over his head was a man in a white cloak. His hands were placed about two inches away from either side of Mert's temples. White energy was surging out of each of his hands and into Mert's head. Mert's body convulsed, and he strained against the straps holding him. His veins looked as though they were threatening to burst. His face contorted in odd shapes showing the pain in his body. In his mouth was a piece of wood held in by a strap. River couldn't take his eyes off of the sight.

Completely focused on what was happening, he jumped when he heard someone clear their throat behind him. He looked over his shoulder just in time to see a club bash his face. Searing pain erupted through his body, and all went black.

River opened his eyes. He was lying on the ground, Azailia cradling his head. He looked directly into her eyes. "My name is Llider. I remember everything!"

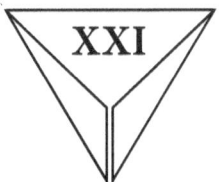

XXI

Llider sat up, the memories flooding back to him. Azailia smiled as she looked at him.

"Llider, huh?" she said, smirking. "Well, it's nice to meet you, Llider." She finished with a giggle. Zeigen was there; he had run over when Llider collapsed.

"I'm glad your memories are back," he said as he helped Llider to his feet. "Come, we should find Kohen. He'll want to ask you some questions."

Llider, Azailia and Zeigen made their way to the field where Kohen was waiting. As soon as he saw Llider, he stormed over.

"Where have you been? I've been waiting here forever. We've lost so much time today." He was fuming.

"Relax, Kohen," replied Llider. He held out his hand, "I'm Llider. Nice to meet you." Kohen stared at Llider's hand, then a wide smile broke out, and he shook it with both of his.

"Amazing! They all came back?" he asked, intrigued. Llider nodded. "Incredible. What triggered it?"

"Azailia and I were walking through the training fields, and some recruits were practicing a certain spell on some wood. When I got closer, I saw the burn on the wood, and something just clicked. The memories flooded in so fast they knocked me off my feet."

"Incredible, just incredible." He looked at Llider as if he were a subject to be studied. "The mind is an amazing thing, isn't it?" Kohen said, and Llider nodded. "So tell me, what do you remember? How'd you lose your memory?"

Llider proceeded to tell them everything, from his forced recruitment, to the strange voice he heard in the middle of the rainstorm. He even described how he noticed the soldiers acting funny. They listened intently the entire time. Zeigen seemed to take special interest when he recalled the Special Training the king was putting everyone through.

"So, that's how they're doing it. That makes more sense," Zeigen said when Llider finished.

"What do you mean?" Azailia asked.

"Well," Zeigen started, "the mind is a very powerful tool. However, the mind is not the brain. Do you believe that?" They nodded. "Good. The brain is still important, as the body cannot operate without it. Now, if you were to disable the brain a certain amount, you could theoretically make people more docile—more controllable.

"This must be what you saw." He looked at Llider, "The Pravicus figured out how to alter one's brain enough so they can still fight well but obey orders without their own determination. This is huge. I must leave. Until I return, Azailia, I want you to train Llider as I have you. We have much work to do." He turned and departed before anyone could say a thing.

The next day, Llider met Azailia at the top of the same hill she had trained with Zeigen on. Llider had two swords strapped to his back that he got from the armory. Azailia's lay next to her on the ground. They stood facing each other, wooden swords in each of their hands.

"This is ridiculous," Llider said. "I'm already trained. Why do we need to do this?"

"Okay, then hit me," she replied.

"I'm not going to hit you," he said defiantly.

"That's because you can't." With a swift movement, she lunged at him, hit him across the arm and bounced back.

"What the hell?" he said as he rubbed his arm.

"Like I said, you won't be able to." She smiled again.

"Fine!" He lunged at her.

Back and forth they went, Llider was able to keep up with her for quite a while, but in the end, she had won. They trained with the sword for a few days. At the end of each day, they would both be covered in fresh bruises.

"This is why we don't practice with real swords." She laughed as she pushed him playfully.

They moved to the bow afterwards. Llider was extremely skilled with it. He had been hunting since he was old enough to hold his own bow.

"Tomorrow," she said as the day came to an end, "I'm going to try and teach you how to use magic. It'll be a little more difficult—you being human—but I think you can manage."

They grew much closer as time passed. With Llider's memories back, he was able to share more with Azailia than he ever thought possible. He was happy, as was she.

"Goodnight," she said as they entered their living quarters. He paused, looking at her. Her beauty still took his breath away. "What?" she said, blushing. He grabbed her hand and pulled her close, his hands resting on her lower back.

"Thank you," he said as he gazed in her eyes.

"For what?" she replied, her heart beating a mile a minute.

"For believing in me and getting me through everything. I couldn't have done it without you," he said softly. They stared at each other for a seemingly endless amount of time. She finally pulled him in, pushed herself up on her tiptoes and kissed him on the cheek.

"Goodnight," she said again and retired to her room. He just stood there with his hand on the spot she had kissed him.

The next morning, they were at it again. They stood facing each other on the hill. "Now, I'm going to teach you some basic spells. The words you are going to use are: *Ignis* for fire, *Hydor* for water and *Erda* for earth. These are the words you use to give your energy form.

"One thing that is very important to know—the energy you use is called your "Lib Fortis", which means "Life Force". Just like a muscle, it can be trained and strengthened. Be careful though; if you use too much, you can kill yourself." Llider nodded in understanding.

"Watch me," she said. She opened her palm and concentrated. She pulled energy and focused it in her hand, and when she had built up enough, she spoke. "Ignis." A ball of fire ignited in her palm. She smiled and looked at Llider. "Your turn." She closed her hand, extinguishing the ball.

Llider stood there, not sure what to do. He opened his palm face up, nothing happened. Azailia smiled.

"Concentrate on drawing the energy around you into your hand," she explained.

He closed his eyes and focused his mind. He felt the wind blowing around him. He felt his own blood pumping through his veins. Then he felt the energy building.

He focused on directing it to his hand. The energy obeyed quickly. When he had built enough in his hand, he spoke. "Ignis." A ball of fire exploded in his hand. It was a perfect sphere.

Llider looked at Azailia, her face was shocked. "That's amazing," she said, surprised. Llider closed his hand, and the ball disappeared.

"Incredible!" she said, still shocked. "You've never done magic before?" He shook his head. "Wow! Impressive. Now, water."

He did the same thing but created a ball of water this time. Again, it was a perfect sphere. The water stayed put, not dripping or spilling over.

"I just can't believe it! This is incredible," she said. "Wait until Zeigen sees this. Now, let's try the hard one—earth."

Palms down this time, he did the exact same thing, using the word for earth. A chunk of earth rose from the ground. Llider focused harder this time. His arm began to tingle as the energy surged through him. He held it a few seconds and then released it. The earth fell back to the ground.

Azailia stared at him, her mouth open in shock. He smiled. "Was that good?" Llider said. Azailia nodded, still amazed.

"How do you feel?" she finally said.

"I feel fine," he replied, not sure what she meant.

"Really? You're not tired at all?" she pressed.

"No, not at all," he said. She looked at him astounded.

"Azailia!" A voice called up to them before she had a chance to ask another question. A man ran up to them and handed her a piece of parchment. It was folded and sealed. He bowed and left.

She opened the letter and read it. The letter fell from her hands as she finished. Tears had already started to build in her eyes. "My parents have been captured."

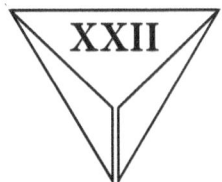

XXII

Azailia stood there as the letter hit the ground, her world crashed in on her as she blankly stared into the distance. She could see Llider trying to talk to her. His mouth moved, but all that came out were muffled noises, which sounded too far away to understand. Her legs gave out under her as despair engulfed her, and she fell to her knees.

Llider dropped to his knees, his hands on her shoulders. She could see the trouble on his face, but she didn't care. Nothing mattered anymore. She had been spending all this time doing almost nothing while her parents were probably being tortured. Her pain building, she grabbed the letter and crushed it in her hand. She let out a piercing scream that echoed around the land.

She stood up, shrugged Llider off violently and stormed away. Llider just watched her go. He knew nothing he could say or do would help right now. He picked up the crumpled note lying in front of him.

Azailia,

As you know, your parents were sent to contact one of our spies. Something went wrong. One of our men on the inside reported last seeing them being taken to Agon-Zare.

My Deepest Condolences.

"Agon-Zare?" he said as he finished reading. He hadn't heard of that place before. Clearly it wasn't a good thing. He went off to find Azailia. He had a pretty good idea of where she would be. Sure enough, he found her in the stables preparing her horse, Prow.

"Where are you going?" he asked.

"I'm going to find my parents," she replied curtly.

"Are you sure that's a good idea? Maybe we should talk to Zeigen before we leave." She shot him a glance that made him go cold inside. Realizing what he needed to do, he walked up to another stable and started preparing the horse he had been permitted to use.

"What are you doing!" she said.

"I'm coming with you," he replied matter-of-factly. She stopped and walked over to him.

"No, you're not!" She began unstrapping the saddle on his horse.

He turned to her. "I wasn't giving you the option," he said with a slight smile. Then he redid the straps.

"I didn't ask you to come. It's not your problem," she replied, her anger permeating the air. He stopped and turned to her, grabbed her wrist, and forced her to face him.

"Look, I care about you. I'm not going to let you go

alone whether you want me there or not. You can fight me all you want, but in the end you can't actually stop me." His voice wasn't harsh. It was calm and straightforward. Her eyes flashed for a second then softened. Giving up the fight, she returned to preparing her horse.

They were silent the rest of the time. When both had finished, they rode out and made their way to the tunnel in the mountain. Zeigen was there as they rode up to it.

"Where do you think you two are going?" His face was set and stern.

"Azailia received a letter saying her parents were captured. We're going to get them," Llider replied.

"Come with me first," he commanded.

"NO! Zeigen, we are going now," Azailia shot.

"Azailia, trust me, come with me first. There are things you must know before you leave." There was no question in his voice. His tone exerted a "no-other-option" feeling.

"I am going n—" Azailia began to say.

"ENOUGH!" Zeigen interrupted her. The air thickened as his voice boomed over them. You could feel the energy emanating from him. Llider was a little taken aback; he had never felt such power or seen Zeigen react like this.

Defeated, she followed, protesting silently the entire way. Zeigen led them into a room Llider had never been in. There was a large table in the middle with maps across its surface. On the side of the wall was a large closet. Its doors were shut and locked.

Zeigen walked to the other side of the table. He motioned for them to stand across from him. He shuffled some maps around, and finding the one he was looking for, he pushed the others away and unraveled it. It was a map of NeaVall, except it was more concentrated on the west side. It was very plain. It marked the basic cities but it didn't show the Drutas camp.

"This," he started, "is our map room. It contains all the maps our scouts have drawn. For the last few years, we have been secretly creating these so we can plan better attacks." Llider looked at the maps, unimpressed.

"Velum," he said as he waved his hand over the map. Lines immediately began to appear. They ran up and down the map, marking different routes that had been taken. The Drutas camp slowly arose on the far west. A few black marks began to appear around the cities. One line ran up into the Hadric Mountains. When it touched a gap in the mountains, a black cloud appeared, nestled in the gap. Another line shot from the camp across to Su'Vasta. Its color was a glowing white. Once it reached Su'Vasta, it connected with a yellowish dot. It then shot up alone and went straight to the black cloud in the mountains and disappeared.

"Amazing!" Llider stared in awe as the rest of the map completed.

"It's how we've been tracking everything. The yellow dots, those are our spies. We can track their movements anywhere. The dark brown lines are routes that we've travelled. The black dots are where we've encountered problems. The white line," he paused and looked at Azailia, his face saddening, "this is your parents. See?" He traced the line as he spoke. "They left the encampment and travelled to Su'Vasta. There you can see they met up with the spy. Then something went wrong, and they were taken directly here." He pointed at the black cloud.

"What is that place?" Llider asked.

"It's Agon-Zare," Azailia said in a whisper. Her face

had darkened and her eyes fell. Llider looked at Zeigen, confused.

"Agon-Zare is a location that we just recently found. It doesn't look like much up front—a simple outpost built into the mountains. However, underneath is a vast system of corridors all leading to many different rooms. What happens in this place we can only venture a guess at. But all we know is when people enter this place, they usually don't leave." His face grimaced at the thought of his next statement. "This is where your parents are."

Azailia looked up, her face determined. "How do we get in?"

"You know," he paused.

"I don't want to hear it. I'm going. I will find them!" She cut him off before he could say what they were all thinking. "How do we get in?"

Zeigen sighed. "Trying to go through the main entrance would be suicide. The scout who came upon this place was lucky enough to find a back door. It's on the west side of the mountain. The only problem is you have to go through a narrow passage that leads you directly by the outpost. Your best bet would be to go over the mountain." Zeigen traced his finger as he spoke, leaving a faint line on the map. It faded away slowly.

"No, we don't have time for that," Azailia said. "We'll sneak around the outpost and go straight for the back door." They continued to make plans until everything was laid out.

"Now, one more thing," Zeigen said. "I want you two to take something." He turned around to the cabinets, pulled out a key, and unlocked them. Inside was a very old-looking box. He brought it over and set it on the table. The inside of the box was lined with velvet and sitting inside were three leather wrist cuffs. There was a spot for a forth, but it was missing. Zeigen pulled one out.

"These are extremely rare. In fact, these are the last three in existence. They are called Norna."

"Where's the fourth?" Llider asked.

"It went missing many, many years ago. We think it was destroyed, but no one knows for sure. Now this," he pointed to a clear gem embedded in the top of the cuff, "this is why these cuffs are so valuable. Legend states that the dragons, when they were here, wanted to be able to communicate with the hierarchy. Together, the dragons created the four gems and fused them into the cuffs. The leather itself cannot be destroyed. The only way to permanently destroy them is with dragon fire.

"They give the people wearing them the ability to communicate with each other simply by focusing on them. It doesn't mean that a person can read your thoughts. It just allows you to send communication to each other."

Azailia and Llider looked at them with awe. Zeigen handed each of them one.

"Now, one thing you should know," he said before they put them on, "they latch onto living tissue. There are only two ways to remove them. You will it off yourself, or someone wills it off for you." He smirked slightly. "Once the living tissue it's connected to dies, it releases."

"So, what you're saying is, don't die or get our arms cut off." Llider replied with a hint of humor. Zeigen nodded, and they slid the cuffs over their wrists. Both Llider and Azailia felt it. Once the cuffs were on, they tightened to fit snug around them. Then they felt a prickling feeling on the inside of their skin beneath the cuff. A chill sensation shot through their bodies, both of them shivering.

"What was that?" Azailia asked, holding her wrist up.

"As I said, the Norna attaches itself to living tissue. The Norna itself is a living thing, to a degree. The sensation you felt was it melding with your body.

"I'll be wearing this one. That way, we can communicate while you're gone. If you run into any trouble, all you have to do is focus on me, and I'll be there," he said as he put the third one on his wrist. His eyes fluttered as it melded with him.

That's all there is to it. Llider heard in his head. It was Zeigen's voice. He looked at Azailia; her face showed she heard it too.

Can you hear me? Llider focused on her.

Clearly. Her voice responded instantly.

They both sat atop their horses as the door in the mountain opened.

Ready? Azailia asked. Llider could feel her determination.

"Ready!" he said aloud, and off they went through the tunnel.

Be safe, they both heard Zeigen's voice say.

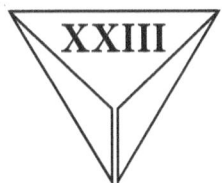

XXIII

They traveled as fast as they could, stopping late at night and starting early the next morning. They had to take a detour a few times to avoid a merchant or patrol. For the most part, they traveled unhindered. On the third night, they rode up to see Agon-Zare in the distance. They found a small area to camp out unseen.

"Zeigen was right," Llider said as he looked over the hill. He was lying on his stomach, scoping the outpost for some time now. Azailia sat lower down the slope. "It looks like nothing. It's just a small outpost. I've only seen two guards this whole time, and they just switch off."

"Well that's what he said. He said it looks very unthreatening, but underneath it's hell," she replied quietly.

"I don't know. It doesn't look like much. I think we could take it," Llider said with an edge of cockiness.

"Let's just stick with the plan, okay?" she said, amused.

Zeigen? Llider reached out. There was a pause.

I'm here. What is it? his response came.

We've arrived. There are only two guards, he informed Zeigen.

Stick to the plan, was his only reply. He could feel

Azailia smiling behind him.

Shut up, he said to her.

The next morning, they started on their way to the west of the outpost. It took longer than they had hoped. They had to continuously avoid detection. By the evening, which ended up working better, they had positioned themselves on the west side of the outpost. The same two guards continued to switch off. They never spoke, never laughed, nothing.

The outpost was a single building; it looked big enough to have two rooms. One guard would be posted outside and one on the inside. They would switch in the morning, mid-afternoon, dusk and the middle of the night. This repeated every day—always the same two guards.

As twilight came, an eerie glow was cast over the outpost. It made it harder to see, which is exactly what they had been waiting for. Azailia and Llider were hidden behind a grouping of rocks just west of the outpost. All they needed to do was wait for the switch and make a run for it. If they timed it right, they would be able to get to the side of the building before the guards saw them.

Just like clockwork, the guard turned to go inside. Llider balanced on his feet, ready to make a run for it. Just as he was about to go, Azailia pulled him back.

"Wait!" she hissed quietly. She pointed just as the guard turned back. Something had grabbed his attention. They both looked. A man was riding towards the outpost, and he was moving fast. The guard turned and rang a bell that was hanging beside the door. He charged down the slope to meet the man. Seconds later, ten soldiers charged out of the outpost.

"Where did they all come from?" Llider said as he crouched lower.

"Quick! Let's go!" Azailia said and pulled him up. The guards were so focused on the man that they didn't even notice the two sneak around. Before they knew it, they were at the side of the building running as fast as they could.

Behind the outpost was a small patch of grass and the mountains. They were trapped. There was nowhere to go. The mountains went from the ground, straight up. There was nowhere to climb and no place to hide.

"Where is it?" Azailia strained.

"I don't know. It must be here," Llider replied. They heard the soldiers meet the man. There was a lot of grumbling and yelling, but he couldn't make out what they said.

"Hurry! They'll be back soon." They went in different directions and scoured back and forth.

"Shit! I think they're coming back," Llider said impatiently. His adrenaline was pumping so much he was shaking. The grumbling turned into loud arguing mixed with confusion.

"It must be here. Zeigen wouldn't send us here if he didn't know for sure." Azailia's voice was getting less and less certain. "It must be here," she said as if reassuring herself.

Llider pounded on the ground by the side of the mountain—still nothing. The voices were audible now.

"What the hell was that?" Llider heard the voices say. They were furious.

"Get over here! You think that was funny?" another voice commanded, this one extremely angry.

"No, no! I swear!" he heard a voice pleading.

"Llider!" he heard Azailia call. "Over here. I found it, quick!" He ran over to where she was standing. Her hands were placed on an indent in the mountain. It blended perfectly with it. The only thing that gave it away was a small handle hanging. If one didn't look close, the handle appeared to be a root growing out of the mountain.

"I don't want excuses!" he heard the angry voice again, followed by a loud crack. The guards were at the door. If they were to look around, they would see them both. Azailia grabbed the handle and pulled. The hatch groaned as she pulled, grass and roots tearing as it opened. Both Llider and Azailia stifled a fit of coughs as the smell overpowered them. They covered their noses.

"Now or never," he said as he looked at Azailia. She slid herself into the black tunnel and was absorbed into the darkness. Llider waited a few seconds and followed. The last thing he heard was the clunk of the hatch closing behind him. Then, darkness.

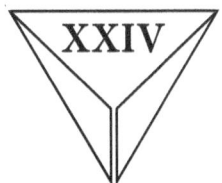

XXIV

Llider landed with a thud. It was completely black in the room, and he couldn't see a thing.

Azailia, where are you? he asked, reaching out with his mind.

"Underneath you," she groaned. He felt a push beneath him, and he rolled over. His eyes began to come into focus. He saw the silhouette of her body lying on the ground. He grabbed her arm and helped her up.

"Are you okay?" he asked quietly.

"Yes," she replied.

"Where are we?" He tried to look around, but it was too dark to see well.

"I'm not sure," she said. "I can't see anything." Llider moved around until he found a wall. "What's that smell?" she said a second later. He had smelled it too. It was foul, like rotting flesh mixed with sewage water.

"It would make sense if this place is a prison," Llider said as he followed the wall with his hands. "It's underground, and I didn't see any place for air to escape." He found a corner, turned and kept going. "Ah ha!" he said as his hands located a door. He cracked it open slightly, letting a small amount of light pour in. Azailia was still in the same spot. She made her way over to him.

They peered out the door. The corridor was empty. Candles hung from the wall at equal intervals. He opened the door more, letting the light flood in. They had landed in what looked like a storage room. On the wall opposite the door was the hole they had fallen through. Llider figured it was used to bring in larger pieces of equipment.

"Which way?" Azailia asked as they left the room. The hallway stretched left and right, each one turning a small distance ahead. Before they could decide, a door swung open on their left. They ran right, turned the corner and stopped, hoping they weren't heard. Llider peered around the corner.

"I told you, I don't care!" the same angry voice said again. A guard was tossed through the door and onto the floor.

"I swear!" the guard pleaded. Before he could speak more, another guard came through the door and kicked him in the gut. He spit blood.

"Take this maggot to a cell," he commanded. "*They* will deal with him."

"No ... No ... Please, I swear." He was sobbing now. "The man on the horse was real. He was coming straight for us!" Two other guards appeared and dragged him down the corridor.

The main guard turned and closed the door. Llider looked at Azailia, a knowing look on her face.

"You used an apparition spell, didn't you?" Llider said, impressed with her quick thinking.

"What?" she said sheepishly. "It was a good distraction, wasn't it?" He smiled. She continued to amaze him. They turned and looked down the corridor. There were doors all along the right wall. Each door had a very small window with bars inside.

"Let's go. I know they're here," she said, determination setting in her face again. They walked down quietly. Llider kept glancing behind them. Each door they passed, she would glance in. Some of the rooms were empty. A few had men in them, some dead, some barely alive. Others had creatures that neither Llider nor Azailia recognized. Door by door they went, until they came to the end of the hall.

Llider peered around the corner. "Clear," he said. The corridor turned to the left. Again, the wall to the right had doors all the way down. A single door was on the left in the middle of the wall. They checked each door as they made their way down the corridor.

A door slammed, and then they both heard footsteps coming their way. "In here!" Llider yelled. They went through the single door on the left wall. Azailia closed it quietly. They stood silently, listening for anymore noise. The footsteps receded.

"I've been waiting for you," an eerily sweet voice said behind them. They both turned. Standing there in white robes, face covered, was him—the Pravicus. Azailia and Llider both froze.

"Where are my parents, you bastard!" Azailia lashed out.

"Now, now, that's no way to speak to me," the Pravicus sneered. Azailia made a motion to attack, but Llider grabbed her, holding her back. The Pravicus let out a vile laugh.

"Come now. That's no way to treat a doctor. I'm just trying to help." He smiled his crooked smile. His words sounded sweet, but their intention was pure evil.

"Where are my parents, dammit!" she yelled at him again.

"Well, aren't you just rude," he replied. "They were here." He stopped and gazed at Azailia.

"Where did you take them?" She was starting to shake.

Calm down. Llider's voice sounded in her head. She took a breath.

"Like I said, they were here." The Pravicus paused again, toying with her. He seemed to be enjoying it greatly. "I had them moved," he finally said, almost nonchalantly. That did it. Azailia launched at him, pulling her sword free. She bounded across the room and slashed through him. He disappeared.

"What the...?" she said as she looked around.

"That wasn't very nice." The voice came from the left side of the room. There he was, standing, looking at Azailia.

"You coward!" she screamed and lunged at him again. Once again, she swung her sword through him and he vanished. She screamed with anger.

"Alright, enough of this," he said, appearing where he originally was. "I've had it with you." His face darkened, and a black aura shimmered around him. Llider felt the change in temperature immediately. The light in the room slowly darkened, casting shadows on the walls. The Pravicus brought his hands up as dark energy swirled around him. The shadows on the walls moved in a way that made them seem alive.

"Arrach Sumon Dre," the Pravicus hissed into the air. His eyes flashed. "I hope you enjoy the Arrachs. They've been quite hungry lately." All pretense of friendliness was gone. He faded away, and with his last word, he was gone.

The shadows began to grow, starting in the middle of each wall and sliding towards them. Azailia and Llider ran to the door. Llider pulled the door. Nothing. He pulled again. "It's stuck!" he said.

She pushed him aside and pulled. "Dammit! What're we going to do?" she replied, panic in her voice. Then Llider had an idea.

"We need light!" Llider said as he raised his hand. "Lucere." A ball of light appeared in his hand, and he threw it at the shadows. The shadows receded slightly. "It won't kill them, but it'll at least give us time to think." They worked together, fending off the shadows. The shadows moved faster and faster until Llider and Azailia couldn't keep up. Their energy was draining, and the Arrachs seemed to sense their exhaustion.

As they slowed down, the shadows moved to a spot in front of them. Two forms began to rise from the shadows. First, heads appeared, and then came bodies, followed by arms and legs. Both their bodies were cloaked in a black mist. A hiss broke through the air, and Llider realized it came from the Arrachs. A single hand appeared from the mist, in it a dagger—the Salareif, as Azailia remembered.

Don't let that dagger near you, Azailia's voice sounded in Llider's mind. With almost blinding speed, the Arrachs attacked. Llider pulled his swords out and blocked; Azailia did the same. They both lunged back. The Arrachs easily blocked them then vanished once again.

"They're fighting as one. That may be our advantage," Llider said. Azailia nodded.

Azailia felt the temperature change behind them. "Behind us!" They both spun as the Arrachs reappeared. Llider brought one sword down on each, and they each blocked his attack. Distracted, Azailia spun around to the left and sliced at one. The face, or what she thought was the face, turned and looked right at her, and then it was gone. They had disappeared again.

"How do we fight them if they can just disappear like that?" Azailia said, her voice nervous. Her calm state was gone. She was concerned. Llider looked around trying to devise a plan.

"The light!" he suddenly said, an idea coming to mind. "They're using the shadows to move. We need to create lasting light to eliminate the shadows so they can't disappear."

"Right!" she replied. They started to cast balls of light that hung in the air, and the shadows began to disappear. One of them appeared right behind Azailia.

"Azailia!" Llider yelled. He moved towards her as the Arrach appeared behind her. She spun and brought her sword up just in time to block its dagger. Before Llider could stop it, the other Arrach appeared in front of him and enveloped him in the mist.

"Nooooo! Llider!" he heard Azailia scream. The lights were getting darker, or so Llider thought. He was fading away. The other Arrach was starting to overcome Azailia. He was falling. His body started to go numb.

LLIDER! her voice screamed in his head. Then a memory flashed.

He was standing on the edge of a road. Trees lined the road up and down. A wagon pulled by two horses trotted along. Two people—a man and a woman—sat in the front. A baby lay in a basket between them. She was talking, but Llider couldn't make out what she was saying.

She looked down at the baby with the look only a mother could give. Her eyes were soft and full of love. The sun was out but being blocked by the trees.

They came closer and closer to Llider, and they

were about to pass him when a shadow started to grow behind the man. A dagger appeared out of his chest. Llider screamed, but no sound came out. Another shadow started to appear behind the woman. Llider tried to call to her, but no noise came out. A dark figure emerged and jammed a dagger through her body. Her eyes flared white as she raised her hand. "Enlumyen," she screamed. A bright white light erupted from her hand.

Llider shielded his eyes. When the light had faded, he looked and saw both dark figures disintegrating. The woman turned and looked at Llider. She fell out of the wagon, the life leaving her eyes. Llider noticed that on her neck were two crescent marks, the point of one in the middle of the other so they curled around each other. They were glowing. As her eyes closed, the markings disappeared.

Llider's eyes shot open. Azailia was doing her best to fight off the two Arrachs but was losing. He raised his hand, and with all his strength, he screamed, "Enlumyen!"

There was a blinding light, and Llider blacked out.

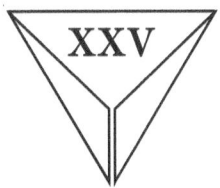

XXV

There was a noise, like a scream but more animalistic. It was a mix of what sounded like thousands of people burning alive and animals in agonizing pain. It had the feeling of life being ripped from you, replaced and then ripped out harder. There was emptiness, not like the emptiness of losing a loved one, but losing everything you had ever cared about. Death.

"Llider."

Another scream. This scream was not that of pain but of worry and grief. This scream was closer yet not as loud. Words. They held meaning. There was desire covered up by despair. Grief.

"Llider."

Movement. Screaming again, more forceful this time. It attacked, not to harm though. More movement. The scream had turned to yelling. More attacks for desire. Anger.

"Llider."

More movement. Calmer this time; the screaming was gone. Calm. Quiet hope replaced the pain. Soft words whispered with desire. A touch. Awful smell. Sweetness. A shiver. Create.

"Llider," her voice said. Llider opened his eyes. His

head rested in Azailia's lap. As his eyes came into focus, he noticed they were outside. They rested in a large grassy field that was surrounded by trees. The air was crisp, a relief from their previous enclosure.

"We have to stop meeting like this," he said with a smile.

Her eyes were bloodshot as she looked down at him. She wasn't in pain; it was despair, grief, anger, and desire all mixed in one. She looked down at him, relief flooding through her.

"I knew you'd be okay. I just knew it. I could feel it!" she said. Her voice was filled with a mix of worry and happiness. The emotions overwhelmed her, and she broke down. She had stayed strong for so long. Now to see him okay and alive, everything just released.

He sat up, pulled her to him and rested her head on his shoulder. She pushed closer to him as if she was trying to be one with him. They sat like that for some time. As her tears slowed, she pulled away and looked up at him.

"I was so worried. I saw you go down and thought I had lost you," she said, recalling what had happened. "After that, it was just so fast. I reacted completely on instinct. I couldn't lose you! I wouldn't." Tears welled up in her eyes again, and she collapsed into him.

"It's okay. I'm all right now," he said as he held her tight. "You saved me." She pulled away and looked into his eyes. The world faded away, and at that point, just the two of them existed. Nothing else mattered anymore. The longing was building up in him. He brushed his hand against the side of her face, following the curve of her cheek. He leaned in and pulled her lips to his. The kiss was warm and sweet. He could feel the intensity from her as she pressed harder into him. His head spun as the kiss lingered on, her hands caressing his back. He was overwhelmed, but he didn't care; he wanted more. It was just now, this moment, this kiss.

Later on, as they were riding, both of them remained silent. Neither wanted to spoil the moment that had just occurred between them. They didn't know where they were headed or what was next, so they just rode south. Azailia was at a loss with what to do about her parents. All evidence said they were dead. She didn't want to believe it, but nothing had proven differently. But she hadn't given up or forgotten about them.

"So...," Llider started, then paused. They had been riding in silence for some time now, and he wasn't sure where to start. He looked over at her. She was so beautiful. The sun enveloped her, making her look like an angel. He smiled.

"Stop it!" she said, noticing him. She blushed and turned away. The way he looked at her made her feel like the most important person in the world. "What were you going to say?"

"Well," he started again as he turned away smiling, "I was going to ask what happened after I passed out."

"What do you remember?" she replied.

"I remember inhaling the mist and blacking out. Then...," he paused, recalling his memory, "I was on a road. There was a carriage. Two people and a baby were in the carriage. They were traveling down the road, and the Arrach appeared behind them. They killed the man, and as they killed the woman, she released a spell which destroyed the Arrach." Something about the symbol made him pause. Should he tell her about it? It seemed personal. She noticed him pause.

"What is it?" she asked.

"Well, before the memory ended...," he paused again. Of course he could trust her. She was on his side. She would be with him always. He decided to tell her. "There was a symbol on her neck. It was of two crescents. One faced the other, and the point of one was in the middle of the other so they curled around each other. They were glowing. As she died, they faded out and disappeared."

"Interesting, I think I've heard of something like that before," she said. "I just can't seem to remember." Setting it aside for now, she asked, "Do you remember what happened next?"

"I remember waking up and seeing the Arrachs almost overpowering you. I remember a surge of energy and a blinding flash of light. Then, nothing, until I woke up in your arms."

"Do you remember what you said?"

"I said something?" he asked, looking at her.

"You actually did more than that," she replied. "You killed the Arrachs."

"I did what?" he said, shocked. He pulled his horse to a stop.

She slowed beside him. "Yeah, you cast a spell that I've only read about. It's called 'Enlumyen'. It's an extremely powerful spell. In the old language it means to 'Illuminate Life'. I read a story when I was a little girl about a group of people who...," she paused as if she remembered something. "That's it!" she said with excitement.

Llider looked at her expectantly. "That's where I remember the markings! A long time ago, there was a race known as the Itari. They were a very powerful race. They resembled both human and elf, though if you walked by one, you probably wouldn't recognize them. The only way to tell a true Itari is by their mark; each had a mark that flared up a certain color when they used magic. Their power was thought to be limitless. Unfortunately, the entire race was hunted and killed. Maybe not though." She looked at him with new interest. "You said that you recalled a memory? Were those your parents?"

"No, my parents live in Mirafol. I've never seen the people in that memory before. Also, the memory I recalled was a dream I had a long time ago. I wasn't recalling the memory. I was recalling the memory of the dream." He was surprised to find himself a little disappointed.

"So, what happened next?" he asked, before he got distracted.

"Right. Okay." Her attention snapped back. "Well, the spell killed the Arrach. Normally it wouldn't have, but they were fully exposed because we removed all the shadows. I saw you collapse. I thought you were dead. I screamed at you, shook you, but you didn't wake up. Then I dragged you out of the outpost."

"What about the guards?" Llider interjected.

"Gone. I don't know where, but they were all gone. But I got you out of there. I didn't want to, but I had to leave you. I ran to get my horse. When Prow and I returned, I put you in Prow's saddle with me, and we rode away, leading your horse. I kept yelling at you to hold on. For some reason, I felt like you could hear me.

"Once I felt we were a safe distance away, I pulled you down onto the ground. Zeigen had given me some herbs before we left, and he had told me that they were the same herbs they used on me when the Arrachs had poisoned me. I forced them down your throat.

"I'm not sure how long we sat there, but it seemed like forever. I talked to you the entire time, telling you to come back to me and to focus on my voice. I was hoping it helped." She stopped speaking. He grabbed her hand. She looked at him and smiled. "Then you finally opened your eyes."

He took her hand and kissed the back of it. "Thank you," he said sweetly.

AZAILIA … LLIDER, Zeigen's voice shouted in both their heads.

Yes? We're here. Llider was the one to respond. He included Azailia so she could hear him too.

Thank goodness! I thought you two were dead, he said, relieved.

We're alive, but we barely made it..., Azailia responded this time.

We'll have time for that later, he said, cutting her off. *Azailia, it's your parents. They were spotted being taken through Itaear in the night. You need to get there immediately.*

Without responding, they dug their heels into their horses, and off they went towards Itaear.

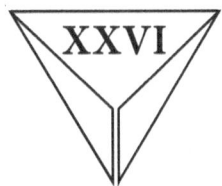

XXVI

They neared Itaear mid-afternoon the next day. They had ridden all night. As they got closer, they heard bells from the town. Azailia listened.

Bong.

Bong.

Bong.

Bong.

Bong.

Bong.

Azailia waited, but no more came.

"Six bells, Llider." She looked at him, concern filling her face. "They're about to execute someone." They raced towards the town. The guards were not at their post. When they entered the town, they noticed no one was around, but they heard a loud commotion coming from the center of town. They continued on foot so as to not attract any attention.

"These two are guilty of treason against the Crown," Azailia heard Reverus' voice saying. "For that, the punishment is death." Azailia and Llider ran faster. They turned the corner and could see the town square was just ahead. All the townspeople were there, looking at

Reverus. The crowd created a human wall, but Azailia and Llider aggressively pushed through.

As the stage came into view, Azailia saw two people on their knees, heads bent down. It was a man and a woman, and just as she realized it was her parents, an axe came down onto her father's neck, severing his head from his body.

"NOOOOOOOOOOOOOOOOOOOO!!!" she screamed as she fell to her knees. Llider was immediately moving. He jumped, landing on the stage. He threw energy at the man with the axe and knocked him back. The crowd erupted in screams, and they took off running.

Reverus stood looking at Llider with a blank stare. Behind him stood six guards. Sitting in a chair, calmly staring at him, was the Pravicus. Next to Azailia's father knelt a woman. She had been blindfolded and bound. She looked as if she had been beaten to an inch of her life. Azailia's mother, he assumed. Reverus turned to the Pravicus. The Pravicus flicked his wrist, and the guards moved at Llider.

With a single motion, he drew one of his swords and killed one of the guards. Another was attacking from his left, and Llider held up his hand. "Ignis," he said, and the guard burst into flames. The other four advanced on him. Two attacked from the right. With a swift motion, he drew his other sword, blocked them both and, with a quick sweeping motion, killed them. The other two also attacked him from the right, but before he had time to move, they lunged for him. Just before they got him, they shot up into the air and into the side of a nearby building. Azailia was standing with her hands out. Her eyes flared as anger poured out of her.

The Pravicus stood up, clapping slowly. "Bravo," he said. "I'm impressed you made it out of Agon-Zare."

His eyes stayed focused on both of them.

"You. Are. Going. To. Die," Azailia said between clenched teeth. The Pravicus moved forward as Reverus disappeared into a building.

"Oh, come now," he said, his voice full of cruelty. "We both know that's not going to happen." Llider kept his eyes focused on the Pravicus as he moved forward. The Pravicus walked up behind Azailia's mother.

"Don't you touch her!" Azailia shouted. In one quick motion, the Pravicus kicked Delia off the edge of the stage. She fell with a thud, not moving. Azailia screamed and charged at him. She leapt right before the stage. "Vincire!" she yelled and pointed both her hands at the Pravicus. A torrent of wind exploded from her hands at him. With amazing speed, he leapt at her and dodged the spell while he drew his sword and brought it down at her head.

Llider launched himself up and blocked the attack. Azailia landed first, followed by Llider. The Pravicus glided as his feet touched lightly. He sneered. Llider lunged at him. Before he was blocked, he sidestepped left and brought his sword down. The Pravicus swiftly deflected the blow and turned to then swing down on Llider. Llider blocked him and went straight for the Pravicus' gut. The Pravicus spun, dodging the attack, and brought his sword around. He clashed with Azailia who had come up behind him.

The two stood engaged for a moment. Azailia pushed with all her might and then brought her hand around and shot energy into him. He was launched backward and landed on his feet. His face had morphed into pure hatred.

Llider took advantage of the moment and launched at

him from the side. With unexpected speed, the Pravicus blocked and faded to the right. Azailia had started her attack, when a dagger flew from the Pravicus and caught her arm. She fell back. Keeping his attention on Llider, he brought his sword down and cut him across the back.

Llider fell forward but quickly recovered. He turned and sent a wave of energy at the Pravicus, who disbanded it with a flick of his wrist. But Llider was on him again. He fought the Pravicus back, keeping up his attack. The Pravicus continued to back up. In one move, Llider brought his swords down with full force. The Pravicus blocked as energy erupted around them, but he held his ground. With more force than Llider had expected, the Pravicus pushed back. Llider lost his balance, and the Pravicus cut him across his stomach. He stumbled back. Azailia was on the other side of the Pravicus. She had pulled the dagger out of her arm and thrown it to the ground.

There they stood—Llider on one side, Azailia on the other, and the Pravicus in the middle.

Listen, Llider's voice came into her head. *We can't do this alone. We need to work together.*

Okay. He could feel her rage. *What did you have in mind?*

"What are you two waiting for? I don't want to be out here forever," the Pravicus mocked.

Llider explained his plan, and Azailia agreed.

They both lunged at him at the same time. But just before they got to him, they went in opposite directions. The Pravicus spun, keeping an eye on Llider. They each sent balls of fire at him. He swatted them away, leaving only puffs of smoke. It's exactly what Llider wanted.

Azailia leapt into the air as Llider turned and

charged directly at him. He brought both swords down at the Pravicus, who deflected them as Azailia fell from above him. Her sword went right through him, and he was gone.

"Azailia! Watch out!" her mother screamed as she dove behind her. The Pravicus' sword went right through Delia, and she fell to the ground, lifeless.

"MOTHER!!!!!!!" Azailia screamed. She placed her hands together and shouted, "Inthaz!" At that exact moment, the Pravicus exploded, his robes lying charred on the ground. Azailia ran to her mother's side and collapsed on top of her, tears flowing freely.

Azailia cradled her mother's head in her lap. Tears streamed down her face and fell freely onto her mother's clothes. Llider made his way over and crouched beside her.

"She loved you so much that she sacrificed herself to save you," Llider said softly. Azailia said nothing, just used her hand to close her mother's eyes for the final time.

θ

Llider and Azailia stood at the top of the hill over-looking Itaear. A massive oak tree stood to their left. The sun was shining down on them. In front of them were two fresh graves shadowed by the tree. A large stone rested between the two mounds. Azailia walked over and knelt between the two. Tears welled up in her eyes.

"I'm so sorry," she said. "I tried, but I just couldn't get there in time." Tears fell freely from her face. Llider walked over and rested his hand on her shoulder. She raised her hand to his. "I'll never forget you. We will meet again. I love you!" She took her free hand and placed it on the front side of the stone.

"Atzen," she said. The stone started to glow. When it faded, engraved in the stone were two words:

Beloved Parents

About the Author

Will Simpson is an American author who has been writing as a hobby since he was very young. He was born in Atlanta, GA and spends a lot of time traveling. He greatly enjoys telling stories that people can immerse themselves into and escape from life for a time!

Stay tuned to see what happens in the next installment of the *Council of Shadows* series

Liked the book? Leave a review on Amazon.com

&

Like us on Facebook at:
www.Facebook.com/
CouncilofShadowsSeries

Instagram:
@CouncilofShadowsSeries

Glossary & Pronunciation

The majority of made-up words in this book are alterations of the older version of the word.

CHARACTERS AND GROUPS:

Arrach (ah'rack)—Irish	"Specter, Apparition."
Azailia (a'zail'YA)	Made Up
Celia (celia)	Made Up
Delia (de'lie'ah)	Made Up
Drutas (DRU'tas)—Lithuanian	"True"
Harrus (hair'us)	Made Up
Heruki (hair'u'key)	Made Up
Itari (i'tari)	Made Up
Kilas (KEY'las)	Made Up
Kohen (Ko'en)—Greek	"Priest"
Llider (LIE'der)	"Leader"
Oli (ah'li)	Made Up
Outen (oh'ten)—Middle English	"To disclose"
Pravicus (pra'vi'cuss)—Latin: *Pravus*	"Crooked" + *Medicus* "Physician"
Prow (prow)—Middle English	"Valiant, Brave"
Salvator (sal'va'tor)—Late Latin	"Savior"
Tere (tary)	Made Up
Vaidya (vI'da)—Sanskrit	"Medical doctor"
Weisen (why'sen)—Germanic	"Show the way"
Zeigen (zI'gen)—Germanic	"To show"

Locations:

Neavall (knee'vall)—French   "New wave"
Agon Zare (A'gone' Z'air)—Latin   "Agony, Pain"
Dagmar (dagmar)
Dearm (dearm)
Devaw (DEE'vaw)
Elaysia (e'lay'zha)
Gusta (GU'sta)
Hadric Mountains (hay'dric mountains)
Itaear (i'Tear)
Jerimati (JERA'mati)
Jetra River (jhe'tra river)
Khali'gas (call'E'gaas)—Germanic   "That must be
                             preserved whole or intact"
Laida (LAY'da)
Mesta (MAY' sta)
Mintual Forest (Min'Tual forest)
Mirafol (MIRRA'fol)
Montege (mon'TEEG)
Opar'Leet (o'par'LEET)
Shesta Lake (SHAY'sta lake)
Su'Vasta (SU'vasta)
The Torr (the Tore)—Old English   "Watchtower"
Tra'vas (tra'vaas)
Trilay Forest (TREE'lay forest)
Ziveer (z'I'VEER)

LANGUAGE AND SPELLS:

Aceocian (ay'oh'see'in)—Old English   "Choke"

Apeiria (a'peer'ia)—Germanic   "Infinity"

Apeiria tre Creatus   "Infinity through Creation"

Apparitionem (a'pa'ri'toe'nem)—Late Latin   "Appearance"

Appagere (a'pa'gheere)—Late Latin   "Rise, Appearance"

Atzen (at'zen)—German   "To etch"

Blocus (bla'caus)—French   "Block"

Creatus (crea'tus)—Latin   "Create"

Cwellan (s'wel'lan)—Old English   "Kill"

Cwellan se soldarius   "Kill The Soldier"

Drievo (dree'vo)—Old Church Slavic   "Tree"

Derkesthai (derk'es'tie)—Greek   "To see clearly"

Enlumyen (en'loo'men)—Middle English   "Illuminate"

Erda (air'da)—Old High German   "Earth"

Freo (fray'oh)—Old English   "Friend"

Fura (fur'ah)—Germanic   "For"

Freo Infinitas Fura   "Friend for Infinity"

Hydor (hi'door)—Greek   "Water"

Ignis (ig'nis)—Latin   "Fire"

Iss (iss)—Old Norse   "Ice"

Inthaz (in'thawz)—Latin   "Explode inside"

Infinitas (in'fin'i'tas)—Latin   "Infinity"

Khailaz (kha'lahze)—Germanic   "Heal"

Lib Fortis—Old High German & Latin   "Life Force"

Lucere (lu'seer)—Latin   "To shine"

Meddwl (meh'dul)—Welsh   "Mind, Thinking"

Nome (nom'eh)—Old English   "Taken, Seized"

Pneuma (neam'a)—Greek   "Spirit"

Pramanus (pra'man'us)—Latin   "Crooked + Evil hand"

Protectus (pro'tec'tus)—Latin   "Cover in front"

Realitatem—Medieval Latin   "Reality"

Reflecio (re'fle'cio)—Late Latin   "Reflection"
Relaisser (re'las'eer)—Old French   "Liberate"
Reparare (rep'a'rare)—Latin   "Put back in order"
Retorner (re'teh-neer)—Old French   "Turn back, Return"
Se (seh)—Old English   "The"
Slawian (sla'wane)—Old English   "Slow"
Soldarius (sol'dare'ius)—Medieval Latin   "Soldier"
Somon Dre (saw'man dre)—Old French   "To summon"
Stuppare (stuppare)—Vulgar Latin   "Stop"
Summon'Ere (sou'mon'air)—Latin   "Summon"
Surgere (su'zshere)—Latin   "To rise"
Tre (tre)—Old Irish   "Through"
Upana (ou'pana)—Germanic   "Open"
Veku (veh'ku)—Old Church Slavic   "Strength, Power"
Velum (vel'um)—Latin   "To reveal"
Vincir (Vin'Seer)—Latin   "Wind"

ITEMS AND PROCEDURES:

Mederi (meh'deerie)—Latin   "Heal"
Mimara (me'mara)—Avestan   "Mindful"
Norna (nor'na)—Swedish   "Communicate secretly"
Pa'Vate (Pa'Vaat)—Sanskrit   "Purify"
Salareif (sala' reef)—Old Norse & German   "Soul Reaper"

www.ingramcontent.com/pod-product-compliance
Lightning Source LLC
Chambersburg PA
CBHW032048240626
47154CB00003B/1121